TARANTULA TOWER: THE ADVENTURES OF SCARLET AND BRADSHAW, VOLUME 4

Theodore Roscoe

TARANTULA TOWER

THE ADVENTURES OF SCARLET
AND BRADSHAW, VOLUME 4

THEODORE ROSCOE

COVER BY

PAUL STAHR

ILLUSTRATED BY

RUDOLPH BELARSKI

SAMUEL CAHAN

M. LINCOLN LEE

V.E. PYLES

STEEGER BOOKS • 2021

PUBLISHING HISTORY

"Tarantula Tower" originally appeared in the September 2, 1933 issue of *Argosy* magazine (Vol. 240, No. 6). Copyright © 1933 by The Frank A. Munsey Company. Copyright renewed © 1960 and assigned to Steeger Properties, LLC. All rights reserved.

"Octopus" originally appeared in the January–February 1934 issue of *Action Stories* magazine (Vol. 12, No. 6). Copyright © 1934 by Fiction House.

"Blood of the Beast" originally appeared in the March–April 1934 issue of *Action Stories* magazine (Vol. 12, No. 7). Copyright © 1934 by Fiction House.

"The Evil Eye" originally appeared in the June 1934 issue of *Action Stories* magazine (Vol. 12, No. 8). Copyright © 1934 by Fiction House.

"Port of Missing Heads" originally appeared in the June 29, 1935 issue of *Argosy* magazine (Vol. 256, No. 5). Copyright © 1935 by The Frank A. Munsey Company. Copyright renewed © 1962 and assigned to Steeger Properties, LLC. All rights reserved.

TABLE OF CONTENTS

TARANTULA TOWER

Bradshaw, the naturalist, went to Central Asia to hunt tarantula specimens, heard the weird story of a million-dollar jewel cache awaiting a discoverer

CHAPTER I

JEWELS OF THE CZAR

WE SAT ON the veranda, Bradshaw and I, cooling off with swizzles and listening to Mother Asia go to sleep. She shut her eyes quickly, night filling the compound with a black that made of our carbide lamp a foolish and valiant thing; but after the heat of the drugged afternoon Asia was restless. She sighed and turned over, yawned and murmured. The dark beyond the bungalow began a secret stirring. In the invisible sandalwoods little kra monkeys chippered. A nocturnal bird fluted twice in the rhododendrons. Insects began a tiny orchestration at the screen, and frogs cleared their throats for the chorus. A chipkilli lizard crept across the ceiling, hung head down, and watched us with bright, inquiring eyes.

Bradshaw put aside his glass and stared out at the velvety black. "Listen to it, will you—A million little creatures getting under way, gathering for a talk. Do you wonder that primitive people believe in witches? In the East especially."

"In America they just believe in a different kind," I observed.

"But this is the country for ghosts," the naturalist chuckled. "Real A-one spooks. Take a night like this. Just listen to it." He sipped his drink with a smile. "In the old days, when I first came out here, it used to get on my nerves. Now it doesn't bother me. Nothing gets on my nerves."

I really believed him, for I'd seen the man shoot his way through a mess of tigers without starting even a sweat-bead.

Cobras were his hobby, and a mad rhino or elephant was all in the day's work.

But the naturalist had no more than uttered the word "nerves" when he slammed down his glass and jumped to his feet open-mouthed. With one motion he threw back his chair, with another whipped a small automatic from his coat and brought the gun-butt down *slam!* on the table. The crash made flame spurt up the lamp chimney and knocked over our bottle of Gordon's.

Bradshaw pocketed the gun and sat down, and his face looked seedy. He was almost shaking.

I stared in astonishment, spilling my drink across my knees. Where the gun had dented the table there was nothing save a tiny brown smear. A spider—one of those harmless little fellows that look like an eight-legged glass marble—had walked around the corner of the lamp innocently questing a fly. I happened to know the brand as non-poisonous. Yet there was the naturalist, staring at the final smear goggle-eyed, and acting as if he'd just stamped out the fuse of an unexpected bomb.

"Those are my *jewels!" said the figure savagely*

"I don't care for spiders, myself," I jibed, "but I don't go into a cat fit when I see one.—For Heaven's sake, what's the matter with you? You just got through telling me nothing bothered your nerves—"

Bradshaw grimaced. "Whew! There's the one thing that does!"

"Spiders?" It brought my mouth open. Not tigers—spiders.

"I hate 'em!" the naturalist admitted in a hollow voice. "Give me snakes, morays, black leopards; you keep the spiders. I can fraternize with everything that walks, flies and swims; but when it comes to the *arachnid* family I'm out. A daddy-longlegs gives me the chills." He grunted. "I suppose it's a complex; and like most fancy complexes there's a story behind it.

"Ten years ago I got along beautifully with spiders, and it was about that time that I went on a trip to hunt tarantulas. Then the hunt turned from spiders to jewels—*crown* jewels!" He leaned forward in his chair, grinning strangely. "I say! Didn't I ever tell you about the time I met the Czar?"

"Spiders? Jewels? The Czar?" I gave him the eye. "The Czar of Russia?" I asked.

"The Czar!" shrieked the horrified Zmeinogorsk

"The Czar of Russia!" he nodded.

"No!" I exploded, skeptically.

"It's the story of how I came to hate spiders," Bradshaw confided. "And you never heard a madder yarn in all your life! When I think of what happened in that tower—that *disappearing* tower—*woosh!* It makes me crawl. Pour yourself a bracer, and here's the story…"

IT REALLY started with a fight—a plain, ordinary gutter brawl. Being younger in those days, and more foolish and heroic, I got into the thing. I said I was more heroic. When it came to spiders, I certainly was. The Royal Society of Science had commissioned me to bring in a special hatch of tarantulas, and was paying big money for the job.

If you know anything about the tarantula you know she's the queen-pin in the spider family; the biggest, wickedest, hairiest devil in the eight-legged tribe. The tarantula has a sinister history, too. In the old days they used to think a victim bitten by a tarantula got a queer disease—called tarantism. The "dancing disease" they called it. The victim had to dance like St. Vitus or he'd die on the spot. Maybe you'll recall that there's a wild, whirling piece of music titled "Tarantella." Well, that's the way it got its name.

Nowadays they know that a tarantula bite isn't quite as dangerous as it was once thought to be. But don't worry. The big spiders are as ugly as the Hunchback of Notre Dame, and a bitten native often dies of sheer fright and so beats the poison on the job.

There's a certain kind of tarantula that lives in Central Asia, up there in that Russian-Siberian region known as the Kirghiz Steppes, about which the scientists didn't know much. These tarantulas were reputed to be the fattest, fiercest and most venomous of all; and they were the specimens the Royal Society sent me after.

To the Kirghiz Steppes after tarantulas! A rotten country to visit for any purpose. It's just north of the Kizill Kum Desert and that God-lost body of water, the Aral Sea. You cut in there out of Turkestan; and believe me, you walk right off the rim of the world.

I chose the town of Tirgiz as the starting point of my expedition, right on the edge of the wilderness; and the minute I landed there I knew I'd come right to the lair of those tarantula spiders. The town was full of them. They'd taken on human form, and were crowding the stench-ridden lanes. Bokhara cameleers, Afridi brigands, Tartars, Turkomans and Kurds from East, West and South, and Muscovites from the North. That town was crammed with the mixtures left by Genghis Khan's Golden Horde, and by beggared refugees from the late Russian Revolution. All of them were stewing and steaming in such a jabberdash of poverty, color, perfume, riches and stench as you never heard.

The place was under the domination of the new Bolshevik government; and to prove this, a couple of high-powered cars flaunting the big red Soviet star would dash once a day through the streets and knock down a lot of camels, vermin and crones. After dark it was every man for himself. In those days a Russian town—starvation and spies and all the rest of it—was bad enough. Fill it with Asians and drop it on the fringe of a wilderness, and somebody'd be stabbed before morning.

I stowed my luggage in the Inn of Tata the Parsee, recommended to me by the police as not quite a hovel. Then I went out for a gasp of fresh air. It looked to me as though somebody'd get stabbed before midnight—my first evening in town, and me walking smack into a fight at the end of a dark alley.

Four big, baboon-faced Turkoman ruffians had a skinny devil back against a wall and were giving him what-for. The skinny chap, hunched over, was all wrapped up in a ragged blue cloak, and the Turkomans were thumping his back with pike-staves. I could see that the scarecrow was taking a beating. His astrakhan hat—one of those hats that look like curly wool muffs—was jammed over his eyes, and he was squealing like a pig in a butchery.

IN THAT town, wearing brand new English drill, a stranger like me must have stood out like a sore thumb. I'd have crossed to the opposite curb and gone past, if the skinny victim hadn't suddenly yowled for help in English. Then I saw that he was a white man.

That was the call for heroism. I jumped into the dust and scuffle, flung punches, dodged a knife, grabbed out my pistol. The four Turkomans faded like smoke in a magician's palm, and I found myself alone amid the alley smells, except for the derelict white man in his ragged cape and astrakhan.

He was all in; I could see that. Bleary eyes winked at me under crusted lids in a gaunt, blue, pock-pitted face. In his chest rattled a cough; his dirty beard looked like an old broom.

"Ten thousand thanks! You have saved my life—"

"Nonsense!" I growled, wanting to get out of there before those vultures came back with a lot of close relations to beat me into a mash. "It was nothing—"

"*Boshe moy!*" he panted. "But for you they would have murdered me. They—they were trying to get the *map!*"

He jerked the word "map" out of his teeth in an *alto mysterioso* that sounded interesting; and before I could wonder what was up, he had dragged himself against me. Putting his whiskers to my ear he hissed:

"My very good friend, just now you have saved my life. I, Boris Zmeinogorsk, Duke of Suslov, former captain of the Imperial Guard, shall repay you well. I will offer you the chance to get a million dollars..."

How would *you* like the chance to get a million dollars? I laughed, of course. Next thing I knew, I was sitting with Boris Zmeinogorsk in a little alcove of Tata's caravanserai, and the Russian was telling me a story. The dirty little hotel was crowded with all the riff-raff of an Asian crossword; opium-yellowed caravaneers in turbans, and slant-eyed Slavs spending their last *kopeks* on garish women.

With all the secrecy of a Wilhelmstrasse spy about to betray grave doings, Zmeinogorsk sneaked me into a deserted cozy corner beneath a balcony. He ordered a filter of absinthe— at my expense—and drew his chair close to mine. He sent a veiled glance over his shoulder, and a covert scrutiny at the dark balcony overhead. Then he turned his eyes on me, and they began to burn like candles.

He began to speak, too. Sonorous pictures wept from his stained, stringy beard. Petrograd. Moscow. Pictures of gray streets under spires and domes, of gray armies marching in gray snow. He had been Duke of Suslov then, attached to the Czar's imperial train. Then the war; Rasputin; Tannenberg; revolution; the emperor put to flight; the nobility blown to the four winds. Zmeinogorsk wept as he recited.

Naturally, I thought he was touched in the head; that he was merely some half-starved derelict stranded in the Russian backwash. But his didoes were amusing; and besides, I had no other way to spend the evening, and nobody likes a good yarn better than I. That Muscovite beggar could talk, and let me tell you I heard a yarn.

Suddenly he tore open his blue cape, dug into an unspeakable undershirt, and gave me a peep at a medal. "You see, my friend?" He squared his thin shoulders. "The Order of St. George—and pinned there by Czar Nikolai's own hand, not twenty-four hours before Russia fell. I would not sell it for a billion dollars—"

BUT THERE *was* something he'd sell, and that was the most astonishing point of the fellow's tale. On the day the Bolshevik revolution exploded, the Reds captured him and threw him into the Fortress of SS. Peter and Paul. By the help of God—and a beautiful woman named Sonia—he had escaped. Russia was upside down—in flames. The Czar and the imperial family had vanished. Boris Zmeinogorsk had been forced to flee, and he had fled across the Ural Mountains and wandered in exile these ten terrible years. Starved and sick, he was beaten and hounded from one end of Siberia to the other, and back. That was why he was as dirty as a peasant; why he—a former Duke of Suslov—

was as thin as a rabbit; why his garments were dishrags and his boots abominable. However, those abominable boots had gotten him into the Kirghiz wilderness one day, and had brought him to the shore of a big black lake.

In the middle of this lake was a tiny island, and on this island stood an ancient stone tower that to Zmeinogorsk's jaundiced eye looked as if it had been there since Time itself.

The Russian's eyes were electric bulbs when he began to tell of that tower… "So old the stones were green and the windows hung with moss. I stared," he whispered, "and the place seemed to lay a spell on me. In the silence of the wilderness I was the only living thing in sight—very lonely, my friend, and starving on my feet. I crept along the shore of the lake, staring at the tower on the island and wondering if aught lived there—and suddenly I came upon a rowboat stranded on the shore. It was a rotten craft, but it told me something. Perhaps the tower was inhabited. Perhaps I could find food here."

Zmeinogorsk said he tightened his belt, got into the boat and paddled out to the island.

"It was scary," he breathed fiercely. "The tower rose there in mid lake like an abandoned lighthouse; like one of those castles in a chess game, it looked. I called out.—No answer but my own voice echoing far and away. It was dark in the tower, my friend; but hunger impels us to cast aside fear. I found a door, entered and climbed a spiral stairway.

"About half way to the top I discovered a tomb-like room. There was nobody in that room. There was only—" Zmeinogorsk reached to hook his fingers on my arm—"a big oaken chest."

"What was in the box?" I grinned. I fancied the fellow would tell me of something that would rival the contents of Pandora's famous cabinet, but I wasn't quite prepared for the answer that steamed from his mouth. He gasped an oath.

"St. Simeon of Vokhuture!—In that chest, my friend, were diamonds and platinum—gold and pearls and emeralds. In that chest were the crown jewels of the Czar!—Aye! And still there."

I felt like saying "Oh, yeah?" But something in the Russian's face stopped me. I wish you could have seen him; ragged and shaky in that horrible blue cloak, the curly astrakhan cap brushed down on his spotty forehead, buttonholing me there in that dark corner of the inn. He looked demented enough. I'd seen the same expression on the face of a New York broker who was trying to corner a fortune. Somehow the smell of absinthe and the sound of the man's voice got into me.

"Still there?" I repeated.

"They are still there. Now how did those treasures get there? I do not know. Some say the Czar and his relatives were shot. Some say he escaped.—The crown jewels vanished with him, that is true. Could he have been spirited into Asia, hidden himself and his fortune in that wilderness tower? I do not know. I only know that the jewels are there—all there, and worth at the cheapest guess a million dollars."

Zmeinogorsk's eyes glittered into mine. "Tonight you saved my life.—I would give you this priceless fortune in return. But poverty drives me to ignominy, and I would escape this wretched land. I will sell you this million-dollar treasure for a mere ten thousand in gold!"

That was what he had to sell me—the crown jewels of Russia, for ten thousand dollars in gold!

"**WHY DIDN'T** you make off with this fortune yourself?" I demanded of him.

The Russian waved his underfed hands. "What chance would I have? I could not carry such a chest. Never could I get those gems out of this cursed country. I am Duke of Suslov; the Soviet spies hunt me. If I were found with such a fortune in my possession, the Reds would butcher me. But you—you are an American! Who would suspect, who would dare lay a hand on you? We can go to the tower together, load the gems in your saddlebags, ride to the border. You can pretend that you are carrying a load of specimens. You have a passport—"

"And you want ten thousand dollars in gold for this?"

"You need only draw the money on the International Bank, here in Tirgiz. Aye—and not a penny of it do you pay me until we get back."

"Until we get back?" I blurted, astonished.

"The lake is but a day's ride to the north," Zmeinogorsk whispered hoarsely. "We can go to-morrow. I will guide you there; show you the tower."

He fumbled in his cloak and drew out a greasy paper. "Here is the map. You saved my life—St. Mitrophane!—I will repay you by giving you the Russian crown jewels—a million-dollar fortune for ten thousand. Not a penny do I ask until you have seen this treasure, held it in your hand, brought it back.—And look!"

He sent his claws into his cloak again, and this time he produced something that set my head to swimming.

A little candlestick, it was, a little golden candlestick. Stamped in the base was the imperial double-eagle, the Romanoff crest. Zmeinogorsk handed me the candlestick under the table, and then *I* was the one to look demented.

"Keep it," he whispered. "I brought it with me as a sample.— But there is more—much more. And now, on your honor, speak of this to no one. Should word of this leak out, the Soviet dogs would shoot me. Your own life would be worth little if the devils guessed of such treasure in your saddle-bags. We must leave early tomorrow morning. You have horses? Good. And now—if you would be kind enough to buy me a meal—"

I bought that fellow his meal. You bet I did. He wolfed the food, apologizing for his bad manners; then he picked up his absinthe bottle, ordered a room, and told me to call him at sunrise, when I was ready. My head spinning like a squirrel-cage, I got out of that hotel and rushed across town under the stars. I'd come to find a load of tarantulas, and I'd run into an Arabian Nights' dream from old Moscow. I'd doubted Zmeinogorsk from the start, but that gold candlestick did something to my head. After all, everyone knew that the Bolshevik storm had blown a lot of Russian nobility across Asia. Good God! Suppose this derelict *was* a former duke? Suppose he *had* stumbled on the family jewels of the vanished Romanoffs? And why would Zmeinogorsk spin me such a fantastic yarn and trust me with that golden candlestick—for nothing but a meal?

It was well after midnight when I found the goldsmith's bazaar. Yet I found one shop open, and I thrust the candlestick under the hawk nose of an old jeweler with a henna beard.

"It is gold," he smirked at me. "But not worth much. Fifty American dollars I will give."

Hence I knew that the piece was genuine, and I fled away, my mouth feeling dry. At daybreak I rode out of Tirgiz with Zmeinogorsk to find the black lake.

I suspected then—and I know now—that I was a fool.

CHAPTER II

VANISHING TOWER

ZMEINOGORSK HADN'T VENTURED back to the tower since discovering the treasure a month before. But the map he'd sketched seemed to mean something, and it took us out of town on a road that might have been paved by the followers of Timur the Lame. Then we left the ancient pike and pushed off through a region of cañons and towering cliffs, patches of desert and patches of tough grass, under a vast, blinding sky. In the sun that boiled high in the morning sky, the landscape was grim as rusty scrap iron. Seven hundred years ago the warriors of Temujin had squalled across the cliffs; the fissures cracking the red escarpments might have been the work of the Mongol Butcher's scimitar. I had the feeling that perhaps it was blood that had left it stained so red.

That Tartar horde had done a thorough job. After Zmeinogorsk's map led us off the highway, life petered out. Only the vultures remained, wheeling along the cliff tops like enemy planes patrolling to sight a victim. We rode all morning at a canter, stopping only for lunch; and afternoon found us crossing a divide that was barren as the Sahara, and lonely as Nowhere. I've been in some desolate spots in my day, but never in a place as desolate as that. The Sahara would be a clattering terminal by comparison. Even the vultures fell behind.

This was the country where I was supposed to be bagging tarantulas, and soon I began to notice evidence of the little devils. Cobwebby holes dotted the ground. I could have stopped and gathered a few quarts of the insects in as many minutes. But I didn't. I was sweating like a wrestler in that heat. Plastered with alkali dust, I was wild to keep going. With every passing mile, air castles went higher and higher in my head, and when I thought of the promised treasure trove, it was all I could do to keep from spurring my mount to a gallop.

The afternoon found me growing uneasy. That timeless landscape was too old, too burned out and quiet. The clatter of the hoofs of our mounts echoed up the rocks and broke a silence that had lain there for seven centuries; a silence that resented the interruption.

A batch of clouds toiled up in the waning afternoon, and although they started long shadows across our path, they couldn't temper the heat. The shadows and silence on those ancient rocks began to work under my fingernails. I began to have a feeling that we were being followed. Twice I was sure of it; and turned in my saddle to look back. The trail behind was an empty blank, under dust and shimmery heat waves.

"Could anyone be trailing us?" I finally asked Zmeinogorsk.

He was startled into blurting an oath. He jumped around; then he laughed and shrugged and patted his weedy whiskers. "It is the country.—The loneliness is bad on the nerves."

We rode along through the deepening afternoon, in that dead country of rocks and boulders and silent cliffs, and the feeling that someone was trailing me persisted. I kept telling myself that this trip was a wild goose chase and that I was the biggest of geese. I told myself I ought to be about my business, tarantula-gathering.

I ran Zmeinogorsk's story ragged in my mind, trying to find a hitch, a flaw. But the Russian was carrying out his end of the adventure faithfully enough—and of course there was the gold candlestick which he'd given me as a sample. Every time I thought of that candlestick, stamped with the imperial trademark, I built taller air castles in my head.

BY LATE afternoon we seemed to have gotten into the very heart of desolation, and I grew as excited as a fiddler's foot.

"How much farther do we go?" I wanted to know.

Zmeinogorsk studied his map and told me it wasn't far.

"Can't we go faster?" I urged. "The sky's getting dark. It looks like rain."

Zmeinogorsk pulled in, waiting for me to come alongside. He gathered his cloak around him, scowling. In the west the batch of clouds had fattened into billowing thunderheads, crowding the sun, though the heat was still intense.

All day, my Russian guide had held down his saddle like a Cossack, riding with Slavic fortitude. Now, with one eye cocked at the sky, he frowned.

"Storms are violent in this country," he growled. "They say that this is the season.—The lake is yet a distance. If you want to turn back—"

As he spoke, a breath of torrid wind fanned through the divide, bringing a flurry of amber dust and a faint, far-off mumble of thunder. A shoulder of cloud touched the sun, and a queer, saffron haze flooded the sky.

"Turn back—when we've come this far?" I snapped. "No. Push on."

He smiled cheerful assent, curveted his horse as if to start on at a gallop. Then I saw him rear up in his saddle, yelling and pointing. "By the Holy Faith, what is that?"

We had halted under a gravelly slope in the lee of a sandstone crag. Hearing the rattle of dislodged pebbles, I followed Zmeinogorsk's finger with a startled eye, and saw something unexpected coming toward us down the slope. On my word, I was surprised into grabbing my pistol.

It looked like Moses coming down that hill—the mummy of Moses, risen from the final dust, and still wearing the shreds of old grave-robes. He must have been crouching up on the crag for a long time, watching our advance—and we hadn't seen him.

Natives can fade into a landscape like that, and it seemed as if this one had been conjured out of the very stones before our eyes.

A flowing, shroud-like robe blew about his pipestem legs; his face was a papery skull, ornamented with deep-sunk eyes, a beard like a white waterfall, and a streaming mane of snowy hair. The blowing robe and the flowing white hair gave one the impression that the creature was floating down the hill. He came at us with his arms lifted toward the yellow sky—and I saw he had no hands, just stumps at the wrists.

That was a nerve-yanking experience, in that silence-bitten wilderness; that maimed old mummy of Moses popping out of a landscape on which everything else but spiders had remembered to die. It gave me a little shock.

I could see that Zmeinogorsk was shocked, too. He wasn't much to look at himself, but in contrast to this withered visitation he was right as rain.

He leveled his revolver at the nearing apparition. "Who are you? What do you want?"

The answer, spoken in Turkoman, almost knocked me out of my saddle. The creature waved a stub of arm at us, and his words, issuing from his liver-red, toothless gums, were cobwebs of sound.

"I am the hermit of Tarantula Lake—the priest of Tarantula Tower. Do not go near the tower, I warn you, for the spirits of the dead must return—"

ZMEINOGORSK VAULTED off his horse and grabbed that old patriarch right by the whiskers, yanking him off his bare feet.

"What have you been doing in that tower, old hyena?" he shouted. "When were *you* in there?"

I knew what the Russian was thinking. Perhaps this ancient vagabond had stumbled into our treasure-trove and had walked off with the prize. And Zmeinogorsk's agitation only served to convince me that *his* story was true.

"Rahmet Ullah!" the ancient screeched, pleadingly, and at the same time terrified. "By Allah's mercy, I have never been

inside the tower—no, nor ever will be. Tarantula Tower is not for human kind. I am but the priest who tends the souls of those who have lost their lives in yonder turret and must dwell by the lake in other form.—I have come but to warn you!"

Zmeinogorsk flung the mendicant into the dust, remounted his horse, and glared down, wiping his fingers on his cloak.

"Nothing but a mad holy man," he assured me with a sneer. "This country is alive with such trash.—See, it is the leprosy that has eaten away his hands.—Bah!" He glowered down at the gibbering mummy. "Why do you warn us from the tower?"

The old creature waved his stumps.

"Because those who die therein may never attain Paradise, but must always return there to dwell. It is the curse of the lake, *feringi!*—Take care lest it fall upon thee!"

Zmeinogorsk laughed. "You warn of ghosts, eh?"

"Aye—ghosts!" cawed the priest. "Sometimes in the form of spirits, sometimes in other form.—In the form of spiders they return.—Those who die in the tower by the tower's curse—they are spirits. Those who die by the bite of the spider—they are tarantulas. You will see them on the shore of the lake, the little spider-souls of those who have died bitten by tarantulas."

I had to laugh, then. Reincarnation is the most ancient of ideas in the East. Hindu and Chinese philosophy is full of it. Orientals think their ancestors carry on as mice and cows and birds; and this old Turkoman mendicant had twisted the belief around to tarantulas. He probably traipsed around the wilderness feeding the spiders, the way the Hindu priests go around putting food in front of snake-holes.

"And many die in Tarantula Tower," the sonorous voice intoned, "for the tarantula claims her own, and the dervish-dance of the poison fang brings death to all. They dance and dance, until at last they have danced themselves into spiders. But the tower is also a spirit in itself. When the sky swallows the moon, the tower flies away, taking those who are in it to Gehenna. When the sky spawns stars anew, the tower will return, awaiting the harvest of fresh souls. Some will be spirits, and some will be spiders. You will see—you will see—you will see…"

He seemed to float back up the hill down which he'd come, waving his stumps and croaking, "You will see—see—see!" Backwards over the crag and down the other side; and the last we saw of him were those weird wrist-bones, gesturing against the sky. When he was gone it was hard to believe he'd been there at all; the landscape had swallowed him, I felt.

The place was as silent as seven cemeteries, now, washed shadowy as a fading photograph by the hazy twilight. I looked at Zmeinogorsk and he looked at me. His pock-spotted face stretched into a smile; but he had to wipe the sweat from his forehead, and I could see that the hermit's wheeze had made an impression upon him. There's no small parcel of the Oriental in a Russian's makeup; anything mystic gets under his skin.

"What could he mean—'one bitten by a tarantula must dance and dance until he becomes a spider'?" Zmeinogorsk spat a nervous curse at the spot where the priest had stood. "What did the old fool mean, about 'the tower flying away when the moon was swallowed and returning when the stars were spawned anew'?—Bah! Trying to scare us, eh?" He hunched his shoulders, narrow-eyed. "That was a madman. Come—we waste time. Let us get on!"

WE SPURRED up the divide, riding shoulder to shoulder, and galloped down a dry watercourse flanked by huge, misshapen rocks. Zmeinogorsk was hurrying now, roweling his mount. He laughed harshly, and said I mustn't believe all that tommyrot we'd heard from the hermit; but he gave me the impression that he was trying to convince himself.

I didn't believe it anyway. I wanted to get to the tower. I didn't like the looks of the sky, for clouds were closing in from all directions, and a yellow wind had started to blow.

We covered a mile in fast time, and Zmeinogorsk said we were almost there. Just ride through the gully up ahead, and we'd come out on flatlands and see the lake and the island and the tower. Anticipation got into me like a sickness; my air castles went higher than a New York skyscraper. We pounded through the gully in a heavy twilight; galloped out on the flats.

I wish I could describe that scene to you. There was the table-land, stretching away and away, under sagging gray clouds, to the northern horizon. A plateau of rock and stone and grass-tufts, reaching as far as a prairie. Desolation was there—with a capital D. We might have ridden out onto the surface of the moon; the plains of the Lost. An infinity of brooding solitude was there.

So, also, was the promised lake. It was like a body of water held in a moon crater, inky with the chemicals of a strange, round shore as flat as a dishpan. A three-mile-wide pond of ink, it seemed to be dwarfed to a puddle in this enormity of tree-less wilderness and sweeping sky. A fringe of salty marshgrass rimmed the lake, like a border of mouldy crust adhering to the edges of a water-filled pie tin. And as we clattered from the gully I sighted the bow of an ancient rowboat, jutting from the shore weeds; and there, too, in the middle of the lake, was the island. Yes, it was! But no tower upon it.

Zmeinogorsk dashed his pony straight out into the shallows, pointed at that distant green islet, and let a howl out of his mouth that must have echoed as far as Stamboul.

"Where is the tower?—The tower is *gone! It isn't there!*"

That was when I laughed. I sat there in my saddle and stared at that little island on which there wasn't so much as a bush, and I yah-ha-ha-ed.

Well, the jest was on me, and this was the pay-off. Away down in my heart, I'd really kidded myself into thinking I might see a tower, and the crown jewels of Russia. Not to mention a lack of jewels, there wasn't even a tower! So I sat there and guffawed, staring off through the twilight at the empty island.

Zmeinogorsk, however, whirled at me with his face a contortion. "You laugh. You think me mad!—You think I saw no tower

on that island? Well, there is the very boat I rowed out there!—
Ha! Come!"

His horse bounded past me in a dust cloud.

"Where are you going?" I shouted.

He stood up in his stirrups and yelled back at me, "I'm going
to find that priest—find out what became of that island tower—"

It was all too much for me. I peered across the black pond and
I couldn't see an inch of masonry on the marooned knoll that
rose up from the middle of the water. If a *castillo* had ever stood
on that island, somebody had done a swell job of eradication.

There was nothing for me to do but chase back into the cliffs
after Zmeinogorsk, who'd gone as wild as a wolf and was whipping his mount up the gully. Low in his saddle, his cape flagging,
he tore straight back to the spot where the priest had appeared.

"Find that priest!" Zmeinogorsk squalled. "Hunt! Hunt!"

WE HUNTED. In the coagulating dusk we rode up and down
and around like a two-man rodeo; but we might as well have
been trying to trace yesterday's breeze. There was a maze of
cañons and boulders, but that mummy of Moses had vanished
himself somewhere among the rocks and had pulled his tracks
in after him.

Ending a rush of futile riding, Zmeinogorsk reined in
alongside of me. He was drenched with sweat and dust, and he
dragged a shaky hand across his eyelids. In the twilight purple,
that Russian looked wholly mad—five hundred per cent mad.

"He's gone! And I tell you there was a tower on that island—
four weeks ago—"

"Maybe the hermit took it down," I leered, good and sore at
myself for permitting myself to be kidded into such a piece of
nonsense. I swore I'd write this day down in red ink; and next
time I'd remember not to go riding off with strangers who told
such amusing fairy tales.

Zmeinogorsk took me literally. "You mean the old priest may
have removed that tower? Impossible! A hundred workmen

would have been many weeks at such a task. I tell you, it was there—standing on that island! And the chest of jewels was in a high room.—If we don't find that priest before dark—"

He spoke too late, for the sky had already become a black shade, tenting low over the cliffs. A sudden gale of wind poured through the divide, and abruptly the landscape was gulped in a whistling darkness. The black came down accompanied by a sudden, cataclysmic explosion, as if the dome of heaven had collapsed to earth in an ebony smother. *Whoosh!* And the earth had vanished. My headgear went planing over the rocks. Zmeinogorsk, not four feet away, was blotted out in a lightless waterfall. Wow! How it rained! Rapier thrusts of light slashed through the sky, hurling thunderbursts against the cliffs, and releasing a torrent. I shan't forget that rainstorm in a hurry.

Zmeinogorsk and I drove our horses into the shelter of a rock and waited, crouching in a blizzard of water. There was another tremendous crash in the sky, and the rain turned to hailstones that shot through the blackness like icy bullets. A violence of electricity split the zenith in a thousand cracks of light. The thunder slam-banged for five minutes in a salvo that shook the landscape like an earthquake. Then it was over as abruptly as it had come. A last fusillade of hail; a torpedo-blast in the air; echoes dying away; the sound giving a final shudder and a last white flash on the horizon. The air was as chill as if the bottom had been kicked out of the temperature. The clouds were torn to pieces overhead, and were running like shreds of cheesecloth across the face of a lop-sided, pallid moon. If the landscape had been lifeless before, it was a thousand times more dead now.

I wrung the water out of my sleeves and pockets. "All right, Zmeinogorsk," I suggested. "Let's get back to town."

The drenching had made me thoroughly sober and sick of this madcap affair, and I spoke in the wheedling tones of a keeper who is trying to tease a dangerous patient back into an asylum.

The Russian looked all in, like a half-drowned rat. But he

shook his watery face. "You think I'm going to lose that chest of jewels?—I tell you, there was a tower on that island!"

So he wanted to keep on with his crackpot jest? There was a peculiar, moony gleam in his eyes, and I suffered a creep or two, right then, certain that the man was soft in the head.

"We saw your lake and island," I said with patience, "and the tower wasn't there."

"I'm going back for another look," he snarled. "I think that devil of a priest had us hypnotized."

That was a good one! I'd heard a lot about the mental power of Asiatics, but in all my time out there I'd never seen it. You know. They prate about the Hindu rope trick and about Chinese telepathy; but the show invariably happens to somebody else. I was sure it would take more than a leprous Moslem hermit to hypnotize a tower—if any—off an island. However, Zmeinogorsk was showing the dogged determination of a batty mind, and his whimsy had to be satisfied. As the lake wasn't far, I ground my teeth and tagged along for "another look." Believe me, I got it!

We galloped our dripping personalities out of the gully for the second time in the past hour, and once more came out upon the shore of the flat, black lake. Only this time the lake wasn't flat. The water was tumbling in Atlantic heaves!

I stared across the chopping surf, with my jaw dropping open. I dug knuckles into my eyes and stared again.

Zmeinogorsk exhaled a gusty shout. "There it is!—The tower!"

CHAPTER III

GHOST OF THE CZAR

TRUE TO ZMEINOGORSK'S description, the tower resembled the castlepiece of a chess game, sitting out there in midlake, under the moon. Bathed in moonlight, lost in that immensity of night and wilderness, the thing was a conjuration if I ever stared pop-eyed at one. I could see the shine of moonbeams on wet, mossy stones, the green vines dangling from the crenellated turret, the waves bounding and creaming against the massive foundations. An hour before, there'd been nothing but a barren island out there. Now there was a full-grown tower, spectral as a lighthouse that lacked a beacon.

I blurted out, "Golly!" The mildest oath I'd spoken in years.

Zmeinogorsk whirled at me. "See? We *were* hypnotized by that jackal priest. Mesmerized! He put a spell on us to make us believe we saw no tower there, when it was out there all the time!"

It was the only explanation left to swallow. That tower was too substantial for a mirage.

My companion was leaping up and down, grabbing at me. "You believe me now? We were mesmerized.—There is our tower. Do you wish to see the jewels—the crown jewels of the Czar?"

I said I did. If a tower could come and go like a will-o'-the-wisp in that wilderness lake, anything was possible. Let this Russian Alice take me through his Siberian wonderland. The next thing I knew, we'd hobbled our horses on the bank and had clambered into the ancient rowboat which fate had left on that shore.

As we stepped into the boat, a big fat tarantula scuttled from under a seat and ran across my boot. The Russian voiced a frightened squawk when I stomped on the spider with a heel. What was a spider to me just then, ha-ha? Later, maybe, I'd think differently.

A silvery trail of moonlight lay across the waves, straight to the base of the tower, and Zmeinogorsk snatched a pair of wormy oars and boated us up that lunar path with a vim that made the water spring from his forehead. Believe me, the whole scene was the stuff of dreams; the ebony, splashing lake; the silent wilderness background; the tower beetling up, with a moon rising behind it; silhouetted black against chrome; magnified taller and taller as we scowed near.

I crouched in the bow and waited for it to go away again, but it didn't go. I began to make out narrow windows, curtained with drapes of moss. I could hear the pound of surf against the foundations, and could see the cavernous black-green maw of a door. In the high, upper reaches of the turret the wind played a moaning chord. Water ran like rivulets of quicksilver down the curved wall, as if pipes somewhere inside were leaking. I swear to Heaven it *was* real!

"We were mesmerized—mesmerized," Zmeinogorsk thattered. "That priest hypnotized us with his cursed story of ghost towers and spiders. The downpour of rain brought us to our senses…"

Yes, and hadn't the hermit priest maundered something about the tower flying away when the moon was gone in the sky? And returning with the new-spawned stars?

Overhead, I saw, pale stars were now twinkling among the cloud wisps, but I didn't point this out to Zmeinogorsk. Why scare him any more? He was rowing like the very devil, propelling our flimsy skiff over the waves with a frenzied strength unexpected in his undernourished frame; and in all too short a time we arrived at the door of the tower.

WE CAME within an ace of capsizing in the plunging surf before Zmeinogorsk could grab an iron hook bedded in the stone doorsill and tether our craft with a length of sour rope. The shadow of the tower loomed over us like a pall, and I confess that my knees wanted to shake when I clambered out of the boat and stumbled up the slimy stone blocks which made a stairway into the arching, dark entry.

The boat had leaked like a sieve in our little excursion out there, but I wasn't glad to disembark. Crown jewels or not, this tower was a cheerless port to make. The tall entryway, dark as the door to Davy Jones's locker, and as damp, boomed with spray.

"Follow me!" Zmeinogorsk leaped past me into a black crypt.

I could hear him fumbling along a wall; then he warned me against barking my shins, and we had started up a winding stone staircase, uncanny with the echo of wind and a submarine growling that seemed to come from sunken dungeons far below. Man, it was shivery, there in that tower!

The stone steps were cracked and crumbly and greasy; it was all one could do to keep one's footing. The staircase corkscrewed up and around like steps going up the inside of a chimney, and I was glad to come to a window where the moonlight sifted dimly through ribbons of moss.

Passing through the slanted rays, Zmeinogorsk looked for all the world like some queer merman caught for a moment in the green camera-lens of an undersea photograph. It was as queer as the Old Harry, in that greenish light, and I heartily wished myself out of there.

But the Russian was taking the steps two at a time, muttering to himself, breathing hard and turning to beckon me on. We mounted another twenty steps, passed another narrow, vine-hung window, and then he gestured me through a dim door.

"Here we are, my friend!" In the crepuscular gloom his eyes were luminous little balls of shine. "Here is the room…"

There I stood, with the prickles on my neck-nape, glaring into a high-ceilinged chamber of shadows and windy dusk that made my palms cold. I wish I could describe that tower room. The flagstone floor, dank under a carpet of weedy slime, was cracked like a porcelain plate. The wall under my hand was slippery as the back of a frog. Water dripped from every crevice and cranny—as if the rainstorm had blown smack through the spongy stones. And deep in the masonry could be heard that secret gurgling and draining.

Moonray, shafting down from windows high overhead, came faint as the light to a well-bottom. The place was so wet and mossy, so dank and black-green, that I felt like some finny creature exploring a new submarine retreat. It was queer, I can tell you that, for we were aloft sixty feet in a tower. Yet there was such an atmosphere of stagnant moisture oozing from the walls that I half expected fish to come swimming through the gloom.

I hung back in the doorway, but Zmeinogorsk didn't linger. He rushed across the floor with a yell, and I saw him stoop to lift the lid of a big wooden box about the size of a girl's hope chest. It leaned like a coffin against the far wall.

He was talking to himself in a disturbance of excited Russian, and when he opened the cover of that chest he shouted at me: "Hi! Look!"

I looked, all right, and I guess I must have shouted. As Zmeinogorsk lifted the chest-lid a blaze of colors tumbled across his boots and scrambled over the flagstones into a pond of moonbeams. Then the moonbeams jumped into action and there was a pyrotechnic sparking. Reds, blues, sapphires, gold; tourmaline and crystal fires; shimmering and twinkling and casting a rainbow shine that traveled up Zmeinogorsk's face.

I was hynotized then, if I hadn't been before. I forgot who I was, or why or where. I stood in a dunce-trance, there in the door of that high, aqueous chamber, and I didn't need Zmeinogorsk's shout to tell me.

"THE CROWN jewels of Russia!" He blurted and danced,

snatching at pieces and holding them up like an auctioneer displaying trinkets. The Czarina's pearls. A picture of the Czarevitch, framed in a thousand brilliant diamonds. The Czarina's gold tea service. A fifty-piece dinner set, stamped with the imperial crest—solid gold. I wish you could have seen that skinny derelict reel off the names as he waved the treasures at me. I remember best a ruby-bedizened ikon that had once been Peter the Great's, a platinum samovar that had belonged to the Czar, and a jug encrusted with enormous emeralds which Zmeinogorsk said had been made for Ivan the Terrible.

What a hope chest that was! Zmeinogorsk clawed through the treasures like a man possessed; then he knelt to scoop up the baubles and pop them back into the box.

"All here! Every bit of it!" he shouted as he played with golden mugs and ropes of pearls. "The Czar himself must have come to this tower and hidden it away. The Romanoff jewels!—*Yours, my friend. Yours because you saved my life.*" He slammed the cover on the chest and started to drag it toward me, where I stood like a statue in the doorway. "You will now give me the ten thousand dollars?"

I couldn't move, but I could croak. I told him I'd give him fifty thousand. I didn't want to cheat him, I said. He nodded, grinning as he towed the heavy box at me across the slippery floor.

"We can load the stuff on our horses!" he panted. "We—"

He never got any farther. He let go of that box, all at once, and I saw him congeal, stiffen, stand suddenly as if a machine inside him had run down. The air coming out of his mouth sounded like the rush of wind from a tire valve. In the moonlight his face became a cartoon drawn with ashes. His eyes took on a painted, wooden stare, like the ogle of a merry-go-round horse; and he began to shake in his rags. He shook so hard, in fact, that he brought a scream right up out of his boots.

"My God!" he shrieked at me. "In the doorway—*the Czar!*"

I spun, grabbing out my pistol. But I couldn't shoot. Not me. My finger froze on the trigger, and my hand turned to ice on the safety catch. Framed in the arch of the door stood a ghostly figure in smoke gray. It was Nicholas the Second of Russia, or I'd never seen his picture in the papers.

On the feet that had gotten him there so silently were the military boots of old Moscow. His baggy trousers, tucked into boot-tops, were the threadbare relics of a forgotten day. He wore a loose-sleeved Russian blouse, belted at the waist by a broad leather strap. A small covered wicker basket was hooked to his belt, and a dagger in a red leather sheath. Medals, stars and a yellow tassel decorated his breast. The face, shaded by the visor of an officer's cap which was ragged and old, was gray, care-worn and elderly, wearing the mild moustache and the trimmed, kingly beard of the Little Father, as his subjects had always called him.

But his eyeballs—his eyeballs glowed like a cat's; and the voice from the beard was a savage rasp. He spoke in guttural Russian, drawing the dagger to point it at Zmeinogorsk and the box.

"Those are *my* jewels!"

With that he whirled at me, striking out. I danced back just in time, and the blade rang on my gun-barrel. Sparks flew as the gun soared off into shadows. My howl was more of fright than pain, for the tip of that blade merely scratched across my ribs, bringing a spurt of blood. Tripping over backwards, I slipped on the clammy floor and dived *smack!* on my forehead. Then I lay half paralyzed against the wall, and listened to Zmeinogorsk screaming.

"Your Imperial Highness! Your Imperial Highness!"

The answer from that gray little Russian pinned me flat to the flagstones.

"Yes," the specter wheezed, "I *am* the Czar—Nikolai the Second, and dead these last ten years."

THE CZAR of Russia! And *dead!*

It brought icicles out of my pores.

I lay on that slimy floor and I couldn't budge a muscle; and I guess he thought I was dead, too, for he gave me a quick, scornful glance, then fixed his gaze on Zmeinogorsk.

"I am dead," he whispered again, "and here in this tower I died—died of bullet wounds on the night I brought my jewels here—"

Zmeinogorsk stood with his mouth open and full of green moonlight. The gray figure of a dead Czar paced slowly at him, knife upraised.

"That is my treasure chest," the specter went on. "Traitor! You would rob from the Emperor of Russia?"

I wish you could have heard that voice; like the talking of a skull.

"No!—No!" Zmeinogorsk screeched like a sick parrot. "In God's name, your Imperial Highness! I did not know you had been in this tower! *This* is no treasure of yours—"

"You would fool me, eh? Lying dog! You came to steal my gems!"

Zmeinogorsk's howling answer took the last ounce of stuffing out of me. "It is the American whom I wished to fool," he caterwauled. "*These* are not the crown jewels! I put them here myself—a month ago. They are but worthless fakes! I hid them here in this old tower, then brought the Yankee out to—"

"You lie! You would cheat me of my treasures!"

"No!—No! It is a trick!" Zmeinogorsk shrieked. "A trick to fool that Yankee. I thought to make him pay big money for the stuff. I swear to God this is but worthless rubbish!"

Do you think he convinced that cat-eyed, spectral figure in gray? It moved slowly through the misty witch-gloom, like a panther stalking a rat. As for me, *I* couldn't have moved if I'd been lying on a stove lid.

It was Zmeinogorsk who moved. A big bawl of terror gusted from his mouth and he grabbed for his pistol. Afterwards I could never remember exactly how it happened, but I know that Zmeinogorsk fired once—*slam!*—and that there was a ringing clang as that ghost-Czar's dagger went flying half way up the wall.

Zmeinogorsk pulled the trigger again, and there was a sickening *clack!*—Jammed! Dropping the gun with a despairing squall, he broad-jumped across the floor and almost got to his disarmed assailant.

Not quite, however; and his assailant wasn't disarmed, either. The phantom of the Little Father flipped a hand to his belt and whipped off that little covered wicker basket that had hung there. Lashing out his hand, he hurled the basket smack into Zmeinogorsk's fright-silly face.

The thing took Zmeinogorsk squarely on the nose. Its cover came off, and the basket exploded a black cloud. Never in the history of wars was there such a bomb. A cloud of black spiders! Big, hairy, savage tarantula spiders!

They poured across Zmeinogorsk's face and filled his beard. They ran down his cheeks and across his forehead; fastened themselves to his ears. Some were small as ants, and some were as big as crabs. Zmeinogorsk's face was just a black, crawling mass of them.

If I live to be a thousand, I'll never forget the scream that came out of him then. If I live to be a million, I'll never forget the way he started to *dance!* In reality, perhaps, he staggered, skidded on the slimy floor. Yet from where I lay against the wall, as though wrapped in ice, it looked as if the man went into a wild, dervishing whirl. I don't know whether that fiend of the Czar started to hum a wild dance tune or not, but I swear to God I heard in the air the mad, exotic strains of the "Tarantella"!

Zmeinogorsk was a shrieking wind, beating at his cheeks, clawing at his dreadful beard, spinning past me and out through the door.

The ghost of the dead Czar of Russia bent to snatch up his dagger; then he went after Zmeinogorsk; and I could hear the thumping and screaming as they raced through the passage. Then the sound of their boots running upstairs—*up*, in that awful tower.

Me? I got to my feet and fled down! I think I fell most of the way down that curving staircase, but I can't remember. My exit from that turret, was no graceful departure, I know. Even at the door below, I could hear the screams.

But the rowboat wasn't there. I suppose it must have filled with water and sunk. And somehow it didn't occur to me as strange that a crude raft of inflated goatskins was tied in its place.

I sprang for the raft, snatched a paddle lying handy, and cut away. The lake was as wild as the English Channel, as dark as pitch with the moon gone, and I had the devil's own time in the surf. But the raft rocked into a current that whirled me away from the tower, and I never once looked back. Some time later I grounded on the weedy bank, in the blackest night I've ever known, and ran along the shore trying to find the horses. I couldn't find them. At last I flopped like a landed fish, flat on the ground, and passed out. I seemed to dream of a crashing thunderstorm; dreamed that I was lying on a shaking mattress of bones. Then dead sleep…

CHAPTER IV

TWO THEORIES

DAYLIGHT WOKE ME; and I shocked awake and wide-eyed, sore from lying on a mound of stones. There was the calm of morning under the sweep of blue sky. A horse—the only one in sight—grazed nearby. The black lake was now as smooth as a millpond in the wilderness scene, and in the middle of the lake was the little green island. There was, you understand, absolutely no sign of a tower.

Well, you can't dream a knife-gash across your ribs and have the scar there in the morning. I caught the horse—it was Zmei-nogorsk's, as it happened—and took a long swig from the saddle canteen. Breathing deeply, I limped down to the absurd goat-skin raft floating in the shallows. I felt pretty sick, paddling out into the lake with the sunshine in my face. And I felt a lot sicker when I stepped off on the little island.

It was a nice little island, about thirty feet round, overgrown with a rank mat of grass. Under the right circumstances, it would have been a lovely spot for a picnic. Only these weren't the right circumstances.

Not far from where my raft touched the bank there lay a trampled astrakhan hat. A few feet away lay a gray cap of a Russian officer, and a crushed yellow tassel. The grass at my feet was simply alive with tarantulas.

I got off that island and off that lake; I grabbed the lone horse and raised dust for fair. Don't ask me how I found the way back to Tirgiz. Love, I suppose, always finds a way. Anyhow, I got into town just at sunset, and staggered into the Inn of Tata.

The missionary doctor told Tata, and Tata told me that I'd been one plenty sick man. A touch of sunstroke, they said. I shouldn't have been horseback riding without my helmet.

The Parsee innkeeper was a good sort of ruffian; he brought me my meals, and he didn't poison me to get my Ingersoll. He could speak English, and he liked to come to my room and gossip friendly bits of news. The last day I was in bed he told me there was quite a hue and cry around town. It seemed that a scientist, a naturalist had wandered off into the Kirghiz wilderness and vanished, leaving no trace.

"But I've come back!" I cried.

"Not you," Tata smiled. "This was a *famous* naturalist—Androninov, by name. A Russian in the Soviet government employ. He was staying at this inn, too. He had the room just over the alcove balcony.—It was all very queer. He rode out of town the same morning you did—right after you, in fact. He took baggage with him, and a goatskin boat. He told me he was going out to collect a basket of tarantulas."

"A wicker basket?" I cried.

"No doubt. He wore such a basket on his belt."

WELL, THAT Soviet fellow was a better naturalist than I was. He'd picked up his load of specimens. I never bothered to get mine. I got the next train out of there, I can tell you that.

All the way back to India I did a lot of thinking. I could see what suckers people are when easy money is mentioned. I suppose Zmeinogorsk had been working his way across Asia selling chests of fake crown jewels to every fathead who showed an innocent face and a new suit. He'd probably been staging those spurious street-corner fights every other week, letting some heroic Yankee fool come along and "save" his life. Then he'd reward his rescuer by selling him a lot of junk made in Japan or somewhere. Ten thousand dollars for trash worth about thirty.

It was smart of him to bait the hook with a candlestick that was the real McCoy, of course. He knew his fish would dash to the local goldsmith with the thing, be assured it was genuine, then take the whole yarn—hook, line and sinker. Those paste jewels and gold bricks out in the tower looked real, too. I consoled myself with the thought that I wasn't the only fathead those paste gems had fooled. That Soviet naturalist had been swindled, too—Androninov, who had occupied the room above the balcony in Tata's little hotel.

I can picture him crouching on that balcony, with his ears out stiff as tin as he listened to the yarn which Zmeinogorsk spun for my benefit, down below. I'll bet Androninov spent the night trimming his whiskers and dashing around town to pawnshops where he could buy up old military medals and cast-off uniforms. He did damn well to trail us like he did, and stop to pick up his tarantula specimens on the way. Remember how I thought we were being followed? Yes, and I'll bet he was hiding among the rocks when the hermit priest appeared to warn us off with his legends of the tower. He must have caught the whole story—and it played right into his hand.

For this Soviet naturalist, Androninov, was the Czar. In that crazy tower—with the moonlight, the moss and the gloom and all—our nerves hopped up to G-strings—well, General Grant, or the King of the House of David, or either of the Smith Brothers could have looked like the Czar of Russia. The get-up fooled me, and it knocked the spots out of that swindler, Zmeinogorsk.

Zmeinogorsk's nerves were in high gear, anyway. He'd planted his fake treasure chest in that tower the month before, thinking it a swell spot to stage his fraud. Then he'd hung around Tirgiz, waiting for a lamb to lead to the shearing. I suppose the town was virgin territory for him, and he'd never heard the tower legend before. He thought he had me hooked; then that priest popped into the picture and dropped a fly in the ointment. Zmeinogorsk's next shock was the total disappearance of the tower, when he got me to the lake. The storm gave him another jolt, and the reappearance of the tower gave him another. And then, when the Czar's ghost showed up, he blew completely to pieces. The cheater had been cheated.

The funny part of it was the way Zmeinogorsk collapsed and screamed his swindle, yet was not believed by the "Czar."—Talk about being caught in your own snare!

And now you know why I don't like spiders.

IT WAS quiet on the veranda, then, except for the flutter of a moth at the screen. The gaunt naturalist had settled back in his chair. He looked tired.

I guess my face showed exasperation.

"What's the matter?" he smiled.

"The tower, out there on that island!"

"Yes," he said, "it bothered me for a long time. It bothers me still. You see, there are two explanations. It was a ghost tower that vanished whenever the sky swallowed the moon—there'd been no moon the night before we got there—and came again with the new-spawned stars.

"That's the first.

"Or you can believe the second—that the tower was not on the island, but that the *island* was on the tower!"

"The island was on the tower!" I gulped. "What the devil—"

"Exactly!—I met a German geologist in Bombay who told me he'd been all through that country up there, on a survey. He said it was queer territory. There are inland lakes that shift a quarter of a mile a year, and show evidence of low and high tide at certain phases of the moon. Some of those lakes are almost bottomless, and in others the bottom lifts and heaves up and down in unexplained seismic eruptions. It's just possible that a tower built in mid lake could sink out of sight during a local storm and rise again with an earthquake—might do it for years. And suppose such a tower sank just to the level of the roof, and the roof was overgrown with thick grass. You might think it was an island out there."

Bradshaw stared at the night-swathed compound. He grinned strangely.

"But on nights—black, like this one—I'm inclined to believe the first theory; a ghost tower, coming and going to claim the souls of the lost.—I never went back to find out. That hermit priest said the place was full of the ghosts of those who'd died there; some would be in spirit form, but the ones bitten by the tarantula—" His gaze wandered to the brown smear which his gun-butt had left on the table. "Like Zmeinogorsk," he whispered.

I don't like spiders, either.

OCTOPUS

*The amazing adventures of Peter Scarlet,
little Yankee curio-hunter, are well-known
to the readers of this magazine. Here is a
new one, blazing with out-trail action.*

Now the green God of Sheba was stalking the night—
With a pistol and poison and sword—
And this road led on to death—
And this to Solomon's hoard

THINGS HAPPENED WHEN Peter Scarlet returned east of
Suez and got off the boat at Terbera. The little American curio
hunter had expected they would; and was servicing his Webley
automatic as the *Red Sea Lady* slid into her berth dockside.

You could smell everything and trouble in Terbera. Sprawled
on the Somaliland coast, its foreshore washed by the Gulf of
Aden, the place was the garbage incinerator of the world. Knife-
nosed Arabs, woolly Abyssinians, Greeks, Spaniards, Cockneys
fresh out of Dartmoor, natives who looked like white men and
white men who looked like natives crowded the wharf to greet
the *Red Sea Lady*. She was a pretty tough dame, herself, and
gave them the bird from her funnel siren as she came alongside.

Scarlet shook his head at the odorous yellow heat sizzling
through his porthole and went on punching shells into his automatic. You could see by the way he snapped in the clip, flicked
open the safety, that he was not unfamiliar with guns. Even if
you couldn't see the four or five sharpshooter's medals rusting
in a box of cast-off collar buttons back home.

Then he tucked the gun into the shoulder holster he hadn't
used since the last time out this way, and strolled out on deck to
survey the town. Colors vivid as parrots in the African twilight.

Greens, reds, browns, and here and there the glint of gun metal or a half-concealed blade. Dock men hollered and bawled as the Arab sailors tossed out the shore lines and the boat's hull ground along the jetty. Scarlet leaned on a stanchion and sought through the surge of beachcomber faces, his sharpened eyes shadowed by the scooped brim of his sun helmet.

He frowned.

The man he wanted wasn't there. And he didn't like the looks of the crowd that was. He stuck a cigarette in his close-clipped, grizzled beard and guessed there was trouble somewhere around the corner.

A hand touched his arm, and the little curio hunter turned swiftly. It was the ship's quartermaster: "Some bunch," the sailor

grinned. "We make some weird ports on this run, but this Somali coast has 'em all beat. Goin' to stay here long, mister?"

"Not any longer than necessary," Scarlet grunted. "Just go ashore and look around, I guess. A little business. How long is the *Lady* tied up here?"

"Only overnight," the sailor growled. "Leave tomorrow dawn. We're unloadin' railroad irons, and as soon as those dock wallopers an' donkey engines get goin' there'll be a row to split your ear drums. God knows why they wanta build a railroad on this coast. There ain't no place to go. Just sand and them lousy red cliffs running off to nowhere. I've been up in them sandstone crags, mister, an' believe me, I didn't stay long. Too much like

walkin' along the forgotten end of the world."

"Is that all there is to the town?" Scarlet asked, gazing off.

"That's all. Nothin' but shacks, beachcombers an' honky tonks. Farther down, they say the coast ain't been explored. Once a year there's a big rush here on some fool treasure legend—King Solomon's mines—buried rubies—that sort of bunk. Then the thing dies out an' th' beachcombers stay stranded and rot to death on this pier. It's a tough spot, all right. There ain't a tougher east of the canal."

"Hmmm," Peter Scarlet drawled absently. "Sounds interesting."

THE SHIP'S engines had stopped. A donkey train chugged out on the pier dragging a string of clanking flatcars. A rusty crane, standing like iron bones against the crimson sky, moved a long, hooked arm over the ship's afterdeck. Stevedores lined up on the wharf, shouting a Babel of tongues, and loading machinery began to pound and thud. Yellow dust boiled up at the sky and seemed to thicken the heat. Scarlet mopped his face and fixed a grim scrutiny on the roof-tops and raffish buildings huddled together on the ragged foreshore under limp gray palms.

Lamps began to wink yellow among the crooked lanes; and the little American curio hunter was uneasy. Those red cliffs swooping down behind the town, jagging along the coast of faded sand looked ancient and mysterious as veils. Silent crags and crinkled ravines, dark as valleys on the moon. The last of daylight lay on the beach dim as an old man's whiskers. It would have been a lot better if he'd gotten here in daytime.

"Yahooo!"

The yell sailed up from below, and Scarlet leaned over the rail. Down on the dock a wizened crone in rags was fishing on the sea wall, pulling in her line. The string came taut out of murky water under the ship's bow, and a wizardish object dangled on the hook. The crone hollered and men came running as she yanked in her catch. A blob of squirming flesh plopped on the concrete. Watery legs writhed and flopped on the stone, and the thing shot a squirt of ink at the old woman's feet.

"Octopus," the quartermaster chewed at Scarlet. "Baby one. They come plenty big in these waters. Lie mostly in the deep coves. Th' natives eat 'em. Big delicacy."

The old woman was stamping on the big delicacy's coiling legs; and Scarlet blew a small oath through his beard. That was a hell of an object to come out of water that had been so blue. By the looks of it, there were a lot of its brothers walking around this place on two legs. He turned away, shoulders hunching.

Arc lights torched down on the pier, and the din gained

momentum as Arabs swarmed aboard and began to heave iron rails overside. A half dozen fights broke out among the stevedores; a black man came running under the bridge-wing, his face gashed by a knife and a crimson thread dribbling from his mouth. An Arab cop hit a thin man over the head with a loaded club, and the business of moving the cargo went on. The iron rails made a crashing like cannon-fire.

Peter Scarlet was glad his gun was against his ribs. He didn't like Terbera. He didn't like his business in Somaliland. He didn't like any of it.

"There goes our gangway," the quartermaster shouted. "An' I wouldn't try to sleep aboard tonight, if I was you. The racket would wake the dead. There's a couple hotels in town, but if you go ashore I wouldn't walk them streets alone for a million dollars."

Peter Scarlet nodded and went down the gangway alone. He was turning up the pier when a yellow-faced dragoman wrapped in a dirty sheet stepped in front of him and held up his hand with a loud whisper.

"Pardon, my frien'. Thees ees Peter Scarlet, the American?"

"Right."

"I have been watching for you, my frien'. A message."

He pressed a soiled bit of notepaper into Scarlet's palm. Standing under an arc light, the little curio hunter opened the note. It was penciled in English and in a hurry:

Scarlet—

Unable meet you at pier. You will understand. Have reserved room for you at Rhodesian Willy's Hotel, within walking distance of wharf. Wait there in your room until you hear from me. Keep absolute silence and lay low. All hell popping. In haste.

Joseph Perdu.

When Scarlet turned around the yellow dragoman had vanished.

CHAPTER II

THERE WAS NO use hunting the fellow—like trying to find a handful of smoke in the dark—but Scarlet didn't like the way he had gone. All the faces and sheets around him looked the same; you couldn't hear yourself think in the uproar. The whole affair smelled worse by the minute, smelled of the underhanded, gave the little curio hunter the feeling he got by watching a moving curtain in a dark window. Why the devil hadn't Perdu given a few details? Why hadn't Perdu been able to meet the ship? What had happened to Doc? Easy enough to guess anything might have happened in this African backwater.

Scarlet hurried up to a native soldier leaning against a shed, carbine in armpit, cheroot in greasy teeth. He had to shout to make himself heard:

"You there! Where's Rhodesian Willy's Hotel?"

The Somali came out of a drugged doze. "Rhodesian Willy's? Down that street. You go thees way, then thees way. Across park. Huh."

Scarlet didn't like it. No taxicabs, cars, rickshaws in this town, and the cops looked doped. Once out of the lighted area of the wharf he was in a muddy lane of shadows where a few bug-plastered bulbs on shabby poles only served to exaggerate the night. The waterfront stank lustily of dead fish and damp weed and old mud. Most of the town seemed dockside where the *Red Sea Lady* lifted her spotty nose above the stench and din. Walking into abrupt night, Scarlet turned "thees way, then thees way" into a district of rat nests where tin pianos jingled and shapeless men brawled like sodden dummies over tables, and shriveled women with travesty faces cawed and beckoned from doorways.

He stumbled over a Negro that might have been drunk or crucified in the middle of the alley; side-stepped a wagon drawn by tandem camels, and came to a park that looked like a deserted graveyard of white men's hopes abandoned to the darkness of Africa. Scarlet slapped mosquitoes and was skirting this deserted garden-spot, passing a wrecked poinsettia bush thick with flowers. He never saw where the weapon came from, but he heard it start.

Zaff!

The little song of a knife, whistling on its stroll somewhere through the air. Instinct, seventh sense, and the training of once used to the outposts of God, Allah and Buddha threw Scarlet to one side. Reflex. The blade razored a slice from his coat collar, soared out under a street lamp and dug itself, quivering, into a palm bole.

Scarlet spun, hurled himself into the poinsettia, dived clean through the mass of blossoms and came out on the other side. But the bush was empty and the park slept undisturbed. In the radius of the mean street light no shadow moved, no sound echoed. A ghost must have launched that blade. A bead of perspiration traveled on Peter Scarlet's forehead. That had been a close thing. Cat-foot, he returned to the street and yanked the dagger from the palm trunk. There were curious inscriptions on the blue bone handle. Coptic writing.

The little curio hunter didn't dillydally to translate the verse just then, but he knew a good thing when he saw it and tucked the shivaree into his pocket. The blade, sharp and needle-narrow, looked poisonous; and from there on Scarlet took no chances. Bravery was all right in books, but his business at hand was stranger than any book, and walking blind into a strange port at night to pick up an unknown deal was something else again.

Right hand in the breast of his coat and eyes conning every

shadow with a gaze as sharp as the thing in his pocket, he strode the middle of the street. The din on the waterfront faded out behind him and this end of town had buried itself in shacks and pulled down the blinds and was waiting for the embalmers. Scarlet thought of Joe Perdu and Doc O'Halley and the octopus spitting on the pier and the knife that had just taken a few stitches out of his collar, and his jaw set into a hardened line.

There was murder afoot in this little suburb.

RHODESIAN WILLY'S looked like the nest for its hatching, and the skinny proprietor with the stained white clothing, the twitchy palm leaf fan, the camera-shutter blink to his pallid eyes and his face spotted with lavender pimples looked, when he came around from behind the desk, as if he'd just been sitting on the egg.

The so-called hotel lobby was deserted to decayed wicker chairs, dented spittoons, tables piled with empty bottles, potted palms and a motionless electric fan. Peter Scarlet had a good look at his host, saw the man was a Spaniard and knew there wouldn't be any Gideon Bibles in this hotel.

The Spig thrust out a hand, chill and moist as a monkey's.

"*Señor* Peter Scarlet. Americano gentleman he called in a while ago an' reserve for you Room Twenty-One. Thees man he said you would know."

"Right. I'll go right up."

"That will be twenty piasters for the night, *señor*."

Rhodesian Willy might have noticed his visitor's eyes narrow thoughtfully as he slapped the coins across the desk. The little American's voice was clipped, hard. "Send up a bottle of the best Hollands you've got. Right away."

"*Si, señor.*"

Two flights up an Arab imitation of a bellhop led way down a rambling hall, unlocked a door, bowed Scarlet into a musty room that boasted a washstand, a peeling chair, a white iron bed draped with mosquito netting, and a single electric bulb in the ceiling. Three windows looked out across a dismal court to a stone building with unlighted windows and a facade of rickety balconies. Scarlet threw open the windows to let escape a gaseous fust and pulled down the rattan blinds. The Arab disappeared and came back with bottle and tray. Scarlet got rid of him with a coin; put an ear to the bolted door and listened to retreating footsteps. Then he went to the wall telephone and lifted the receiver to make certain the thing worked. After which he poured a stiff glass and took four fingers straight.

Scarlet felt uneasy.

He drew the automatic from his holster and placed it handy on the wash stand. He shucked his damp linen coat and hung it on the back of the chair, cursing quietly at the scored collar. Then he drew two cablegramme letters from the inner pocket and sat down to read. He must have read them a hundred times on the mail boat down. Dated a month apart; the little curio hunter had received them in New York, back in the States. As he re-read them now the line of his jaw did not soften, and his diamond blue eyes receded under knitted brows. The first one read:

Peter:

We've struck the mine. Quarter million at least. Amulets, figurines, jewelled plate, antedating Egypt. Coptic inscriptions. Dangerous stuff, too. Say there's a curse on man who finds it. Knife thrown at me other night. Joe worried, but he's been a brick. Home soon with my share as leaving camp for Terbera tonight. Rich for both of us.

Doc.

The second cable letter said:

Peter:

For God's sake come Terbera at once. Situation bad. Afraid something has happened to your cousin. Doc has disappeared. Need your help. Come quickly.

Joe Perdu.

Those were the letters that had brought Peter Scarlet from his quiet retirement in New York to Rhodesian Willy's Hotel in Terbera, Somaliland.

CHAPTER III

THEY HAD BEEN together back in the red days of '18. Scarlet and his cousin Doc O'Halley and the secret service man, Perdu. Scarlet had been American attaché to the British intelligence corps solving ciphers. Doc had been patching them up in the field hospitals. Perdu had been in active service at Istanbul. But an air raid, simultaneous with a surprise charge of Turks had caught them together in a shattered café. Doc had crawled down a flaming stairway to save Perdu, flattened with sharpshooter's lead in his side; and Scarlet had dragged the lot of them to cover. Touch and go, and Perdu would have died if Doc hadn't slaved six nights running with all his medical skill to save him.

"Doc," Perdu had told Peter Scarlet's comrade and cousin, "I owe you my life. If we ever get out of this war you'll hear from me."

But Perdu had disappeared at the close of the war, and they thought he had forgotten. Doc had gone to New York to resume his medical practice; Peter Scarlet had decided it was time for a sane and healthy retirement. Then, after ten years' silent absence, Joe Perdu had turned up in America; charged into Doc's office with wild news.

"Doc, I've been in Africa and located something big. Treasure of the hottest kind. Man, did you ever hear of the Queen of Sheba? Did you ever hear of Solomon's temple and the forgotten mines? I got maps, everything—everything but dough. If you can stake the expedition—"

He went into details.

It would be like rolling off a log. Doc could take his medical kit along with him and pretend to be studying sleeping sickness or African physiology. Perdu would run the digging end of it. They'd have to work strictly sub-rosa—and would Peter Scarlet join the hunt?

"Not on your life," the little curio hunter had announced. "No more of these hare-brained outtrails for me. I'm through. Good luck to both of you. Joe, I don't care what you do, but take care of that sawbones cousin of mine."

"Doc will be safe with me," Perdu had laughed, "as in God's pocket. This is big stuff, Peter. We're comin' back rich."

But what had come back were the two cabled letters—Doc's, then Perdu's....

In the heat-stifled hotel room, while bugs burned and dropped from the overhead bulb, Peter Scarlet read the letters again. Then he dragged from his pocket the note he'd been handed at the pier, and scrutinized the writing. Its broad scrawl was undoubtedly Perdu's with that flaring autograph. The little curio hunter remembered the hand from war correspondence in Palestine. And that was all he had to go on. The two cables, and the note at the pier. Doc had disappeared. Hell was popping. They'd uncovered the legendary treasure, and something was striking from behind the curtains.

"If I only had a hint," Scarlet snarled. "That knife in the park—"

HE PICKED the weapon from his coat; bent his eyes close to the oddly-traced bone handle. With a pencil he outlined the faded hieroglyphics; the knife shook a little in his palm. This writing was older than cuneiform, old as dust fallen in the twilight of history. Any museum would give plenty for such a blade. Peering, Scarlet slowly spelled out the translation on the bone handle. As he read the words a mist came on his forehead and his voice muttered out in his beard.

> Feel of this blade
>   And remember no more—
> For the Green God of Sheba
>   Has knocked at your door—

Yes, and he'd come mighty close to "feeling" that blade and not remembering any more. The Green God of Sheba! The name blurted through his teeth. There weren't many people living who knew of the Green God of Sheba, but Scarlet had heard the ancient legend. The bumboat man at Jibuti had told him the story, and the bumboat man was black as the ace of clubs and turned pretty gray around the gills as he told it. King Solomon's thousand wives had prayed to the Green God, and the Queen of Sheba had piled her pearls at his shrine. Worse than the Green Goddess of Nepal was this ancient African deity of death. Eight arms he had, and a face no human could look upon, and it was said he rose from the sea at moon dark and feasted on eight victims at a time. Half man, half octopus. The god who guarded the lost mines of Solomon. Once he knocked on your door, said the bumboat man at Jibuti, you were a goner.

He'd come pretty close to knocking on Peter Scarlet's "door," and the little American curio hunter put the knife away with a curse, sponged sweat from his throat and stood up, reaching for the gin bottle.

"By God, if anything like that has happened to old Doc—"

Smash! A splintering crackle; a low whistling through the air. Bottle and contents burst to a glassy shower in Scarlet's hand. Something struck *thud!* in the wall beyond him, leaving a black worm-hole in the plaster. The little American curio hunter fell like a log, hitting the floor with a crash.

HE WASN'T dead, though the fall bruised his left elbow and brought a shower of dust and brown lizards down from the ceiling. Fast as a panther Scarlet slithered to the washstand, snatched the pistol, spun and sprang in a low crouch to the sill of the middle window.

The rattan blind had been punctured; the thin bamboo wood

broken inward around a bullet-hole. The little American curio hunter let a soft oath through clenched teeth. He should have known his shadow would outline him on that window blind.

Flattened against the sill, he peered through the crack where screen touched window-side and sent a roving, slit-eyed gaze out across the dark court, searching over the face of the black building beyond. The whole building was swaddled in night; no shadow in the court moved. Peter Scarlet had fought like this before. Someone *was* over there. Pupils contracted, eyes pointed to needles, the little curio hunter detected the first movement on the roof of the building opposite. The black silhouette of a head cautiously upraised above the top balcony. Moonlight glinting darkly on the barrel of a long rifle.

Slam! Flash! Scarlet's automatic squirted white flame; the crash rebounded in the court like a thunderclap. The head wobbled, then sat still like a cabbage perched on the edge of the distant roof. Instantly Scarlet was sorry he'd killed the man. Should have winged him on the scalp, then dashed out to trail the blood. Out in the dark sounded the scurry of fleeing boots. That devil over there had an ally—which meant one down and one to go. Or maybe a hundred, from the racket outside Room Twenty-one.

Boots thumped and echoed in the long hallway. Voices cursed and called. With a quick, soundless stride Scarlet reached the wall, snapped out the overhead light, slid against the washstand and waited, fondling his gun. Knuckles began a hysterical hulla-baloo on the door.

"Who's outside?" Scarlet hailed.

"Rhodesian Willy. I hear noise downstair'. Theenk maybe it shots, big noise, somebody he fall. *Por Dios!*"

"There were two shots fired out there in that court," the curio hunter rasped, "and when the first one was fired I was in bed. Knocked over my chair and a tray of glasses jumping up in the dark. Couldn't see anything. What's going on in this hell hole around here?"

It was dark as a whale hole in the room. Drugged in hot black thick as a hat. If anybody started shooting now, Scarlet whispered to himself, that Spig outside the door would get it right through the panels, his complexion ruined for good and ques-

tions asked afterwards. But the hotel keeper's voice was scared, his words came whinnying through the stale wood.

"Sacred family, I know not what goes on. Thees Somali soldiers. Drunk perhaps! *Bandido!* The town is overflowed weeth renegades!" The voice trailed away, chattering like an excited parrot. "I go to call the police—"

The rumpus in the hall was quieting. Somewhere doors banged. Scarlet dragged a cuff across a wet forehead, holstering the automatic, trying to think. Once the police got here and they might spot that corpse on the roof. Be the devil to pay. The little American paced the floor in a dark well of fury. Twice in two hours the reaper's scythe had shaved him close; his coming to Terbera was known and not wanted. Enemies a possibility from

Fighting with every ounce of power in his frame, Scarlet battled to break the grip of those terrible, boneless arms

any quarter, death the game. Bandits after the fortune Doc and Joe had found? Priests of African sorcery out to guard ancient secrets? Had they got Doc? Were they closing in on Perdu?

Stepping blind at night into a foreign port imbued with mystery and the enemy holding all the cards gave a man nothing to put his teeth into. Maybe he should call the police, himself. But the black police in these lands Back of Beyond were little better than thuggee gangs, and Perdu had warned him to lay low, told him to wait in the room until further word. A mouse rattled in the wall, and Scarlet whirled in a crouch, gun swinging.

THE PHONE'S bell blurted shrill as an alarm, drilling the blue-blackness with sound. *Cllllaring!* Jumping for the wall, Scarlet snatched the receiver. The cry came faint and far away through fizzing wires.

"Peter! Peter Scarlet! Is that you?"

"Perdu!" His lips snarled close to the mouthpiece. "Joe!"

"Yes, yes! God, I'm glad to hear your—"

"Where's Doc?" Scarlet bit out. "What's happened?"

Perdu's voice shook. "I wish to heaven I knew. Peter, he's vanished like I told you in my cable. Gone. He packed his share of the—the find and left camp and went to Terbera. I should have gone with him but I wasn't ready to leave. He went alone; said he'd be all right; anxious to get to the States. Nobody else knew about our discovery. Just the two of us working alone. He reached Terbera; sent a message and said he was sailing on the next boat. I went down to the town to see him off and he wasn't there. Couldn't find hide or hair of him. Nobody had seen him. I asked everywhere. Nobody could remember him or anything. His luggage, every sign of him was gone."

"Did you look? *Look?*"

"I—I've hunted myself sick—"

"He said a knife had been thrown at him."

"So there was. One night. We never knew who did it. Now

they're being thrown at me. Other things have happened. Strange things."

Scarlet's fist was sweating on the receiver. "Where are you now, Perdu."

"At the temple—the Solomon temple. At our camp. I got to town this afternoon before your boat came in and had just time to smuggle you that message."

"I've been shot at," Scarlet swore. "Somebody flung a knife. If anything's happened to Doc I'll tear this town apart, Perdu."

"My God! Then they know you're here—"

"Who's *they?* Speak up, Perdu. I can't hear you."

"Listen," Perdu was crying. "I'm in a telephone station. About two miles from camp. I can't talk to you, you understand? Get it? Can't talk. I'm going right back to our camp. Can you come right away?"

"Faster. How far? Where?"

"You've got to come quick or it may be too late. Hurry. Hurry, in God's name. You can get a horse at the hotel. Take the highway south to Ras Harar. Only one road. Along the coast. Ten miles. Then into the red cliffs. Got it?"

"Right."

"Follow the sandstone road by the old Portuguese lighthouse. You go into crags and through a narrow divide by the sea. You can't miss. About five miles farther you come to a ravine—an ancient quarry. You'll see my horses there. Temple standing on the other side. You have to go on foot across a rope bridge. Tricky business."

"Rope bridge?"

"You'll see it swinging across the ravine. We've been camping in the ruined temple. You'll see. I'll be there waiting. Peter, you've got to reach me just as fast as you can. Ride like hell. I'm being shadowed right now. My God! Did you ever hear of," the voice at the far end of the wire dropped low, "Peter, did you ever hear of the—the Green God of Sheba? Eight arms? No face? Monstrous green body! No, I'm not drunk! It—it's after me I

You've got to get here! Our only chance to save Doc. Can't tell you more. Got to go! Hurry—"

The phone clicked. The little American curio hunter sprang for the door, snatching for his helmet and grabbing out his gun.

CHAPTER IV

AT THE LOWER landing he stopped up short with an oath. Sudden shouting clamored in the night, boiled in echo around the hotel. The lobby doors burst open, spilling a batch of police, native *askaris* in khaki uniforms, black faces grinning under red tarbooshes, eyes wild. An English officer with a German military mustache plunged in the lead, brandishing a revolver. Rhodesian Willy came ratting around from behind his desk, hands semaphoring, pointing up the stairs and blurting a spate of Spig English. The bobbies saw Scarlet and started a rush at the stairway. The Tommy officer pointed his pistol at the curio hunter.

"You, there! In the governor's name! Stand where you are!"

The little American curio hunter's mouth made a horizontal wrench in his beard. "The governor," he drawled quietly, "can go write his name on a wall."

He didn't stand where he was. Going sideways, he dropped over the banisters, vaulted a rubber plant, circled the lobby desk in a bound. The *askaris* opened mouths like watermelons and piled at him across the floor. The Tommy captain bellowed orders. Rhodesian Willy stood against the newel post opening a jack-knife in quick, lemon-colored hands. Swinging from the floor, Scarlet tapped the hotel maestro a smart crack on the forehead. The Spaniard fell with another lavender bump in his facial repertoire.

The room shook with sound. An excitable native patrolman

57

let fly with his carbine, put a bullet through the English officer's helmet and another in the wall clock behind the desk. Peter Scarlet saw the hour was ten, and he couldn't wait. Jaw clamped like a nutcracker, he mowed through the pile-up of policemen, clapping black faces with his pistol barrel, ducking teeth and blows. Hands grabbed as he spun through the bamboo doors, ripped his coat up the back seam. A soldier ran at him across the veranda. Scarlet kicked the fellow's bayonet and kept his foot going deep into a scrawny stomach, sending the black heels over head like an acrobatic toy. Somehow or other he was in the dark and dust of the street.

By the sound, all of Somaliland was after him; would have nailed him if it hadn't been for the motorcycle. An officer's machine parked at the curb. Scarlet hadn't seen one since the war, but he'd handled them in those days and it was any horse in this race. A leap to straddle the machine. A fast kick at the starting pedal. The engine uncorked a roar. Twirling the handle-grips, Scarlet launched across the roadway, took a corner full gun, leg out stiff and boot ripping through earth to keep from capsizing, and whammed down the highway, jumping curbstones. Hotel and pandemonium made a fadeaway in the dust swirl behind.

Bent over the bars, the little curio hunter blasted a path through the night, took another corner on high, just missed amputating the foot from a stork-legged native squatting in a gutter. Slamming under a street arch, he switched on the head-lamp just in time to discover a broad turnpike stretching off to starboard and a rickety signpost that pointed: *Ras Harar. 14 K.S.*

Touch and go skidding over ruts on this unfamiliar, night-blotted road that might have been the path to Cerebus. Treacherous with sand holes and cartwheel grooves, the roadway curved like the back of a tortured snake into a night the thickest Scarlet had ever known, but he drove the machine to the last notch, racketing down a corridor of pitch with stars like pale holes and a thin Moslem moon sailing the indigo overhead and the town vanishing behind in gas fumes and dust.

"Hurry!" Perdu had cried. "Our last chance to save Doc!"

Above the staccato rataplan of the motorcycle exhaust the cry beat time through Peter Scarlet's head and held his fists sweating on the twisted grips. Two miles of steeplechase turns in almost as many minutes and he was topping a rise, able to glance back and see the town on the curve of the shoreline, the wink of clustered lamps, the miniature lights of the vessel loading on the waterfront and the endless sweep of the tropic gulf.

If the petrol held out he'd make it fast. The headlamp swung a white blaze around the turns, picking out sandstone cliffs, patches of beach where water creamed, incidental thatch-roofed huts. A glimpse of wattle walls, mud ovens like giant beehives, a monkey scampering for cover. Cats flashed green eyes vanishing in roadside thickets and the little curio hunter remembered he was in a country of lions. But he wasn't slowing.

TEN MILES..... He roared through Ras Harar, a smell in the dark. Grass huts and a scattering handful of natives that fled, screaming, into mud lanes. A town that vanished as quickly as it had come. The headlight picked out a turn, there was a stretch of stony beach, a white shaft, tall as a monument, rearing suddenly and ghostly in the darkness. The Portuguese lighthouse, a token for mariners in the days of Prester John. On that African coast, its beacon long since blind of age, the thing was a wraith in stone. Nobody had been in that turret for a hundred years. The slamming echo of the motorcycle engine spattered up the lonely white wall.

Slam! Crack! Crack! That wasn't motorcycle explosions, and the wall wasn't so lonely. Fireflies danced on the deck of the lighthouse turret, squirts of pumpkin-colored flame in the gloom. Balls of dust jumped in the road around Scarlet's machine. A lead bee whined by his ear and over his left shoulder another made a brief twang in the air like a picked mandolin string.

Speeding under the steep wall, Scarlet flattened on the handlebars, leaning far inward on a sharp bend. Hollering split the night; the swinging headlamp fell in a sweeping ray straight on a band of savages crowding the road from ditch to ditch.

Spears waving at the stars. Coal-shiny bodies capering behind lion-hide shields. Bird-like topknots of colored feathers waving above twisted faces streaked with diabolic smears of paint. Bullets from above and the savage crowd ahead. The mob jumping and hooting like monkeys yanked on invisible strings.

Swinging in saddle, Scarlet unlashed four shots at the high tower. A throaty scream sopranoed up from the turret, and a black shadow dived down from the sky, hitting the lighthouse base and bouncing a yard in the air. At the same time Scarlet's machine struck the traffic jam. Yells and spears sailed around his face in a pinwheel spin, and a dripping Somali savage somersaulted over the handlebars, turned in midair, lit in the dust behind the rear tire. Then the rumpus was gone as he cut the trail in clean wind through a narrow divide, his engine popping like a machine-gun, the exhaust puncturing the black with yellow flame.

Two miles farther, pounding through the velvet with a smell of salt and sea in his nostrils and the crags a jagged outline against the moon, he was riding down the rim of Nowhere, his engine smashing the silence for the first time.

The rind of moon slipped over a dim escarpment, silvering the landscape to the unreal quality of a faded photograph. The sea was invisible beyond a ridge of rock; perhaps the world ended there and the void began. Terbera and the lighthouse, policemen and ambush seemed a ten year's march away; this was the heart of Africa, the place where the universe began and was left unfinished. A man on a motorcycle was lonely in that spot of coastline, even if he clutched a heated Webley in his grip. The road was a warning against travelers. Stones and sand spurted from the wheels of the machine; the road dived sharply between two mountainous boulders; Scarlet swayed on the turn, glimpsed a pair of horses grazing under a hunchbacked palm, saw the landscape fall away to vacancy under the racing wheel beneath his headlight.

With a strangled yell he tramped on the brake. The cycle bucked out from under him, spun roaring in the dirt, tumbled and banged into a ditch. The little American curio hunter went hurtling through a haze of smoke, sprawled flat, and landed, gasping a lungful of ice, on the rim of close death.

What he saw in that emptiness of moonlit space brought the sweat bubbling out on his forehead and an oath knotting his tongue.

CHAPTER V

PETER SCARLET SHOUTED a whisper. He yanked himself back, clawing the ground. He got to his overturned motorcycle, switched off the gas, then crawled forward for another look. A giant's scimitar had gashed that ravine from the landscape in the days when the dinosaurs walked. Another foot forward and he'd have gone down a straight drop of seventy-five feet, a wall as sheer, smooth and precipitous as black glass.

Moonbeams fell far down the wall and touched the surface of a deep pool, flat as a pond of ink. From above it was like staring down a well. Stars made a pattern of phantom twinkles on the black water, and the ravine walls were quarried out and undercut so that the water lay as in a bottomless and monstrous pitcher with glasseous sides. Peter Scarlet didn't like that quarry. Heights made his sweat run. That canyon was too sheer, too lonely. From the shadowed depths far below came a subterranean gurgling, faint as the secret leaking of blood. But it was the bridge that brought an ache to the roots of the little curio hunter's hair. Seventy-five feet sheer that gash dropped, and the same distance across from rim to rim.

The rope bridge stretching across the gap looked insecure as a span of spider web; hempen strands moored to posts on either side. A Jacob's ladder with rope rungs that were nothing but stepping-stones in space, sagging dangerously in the middle and a single hand-rope running along one side. Scarlet didn't like the looks of that bridge with the water far below.

Or the black ruin lifted against the sky on the opposite ledge. Stone steps and massive half-fallen pillars clothed in a drape of weeds. The ruptured masonry had toppled when the pyramids were new; a flight of crumpled steps led to a doorway that was forbidding and murky as the entrance to a catacomb. Behind this architectural wreckage grew fantastic sentinels, lofty eucalyptus trees like mast-heads under the sky. The place smelled of antiquity and a silence that got in the little curio hunter's hair. The sight of the ravine and the frail trestle made his teeth want to clack and a mist dampen his forehead.

Then, just as he was pulling his nerves together, a hollering banshee wail sailed out of the temple door and sent him jangling again.

"Help! Awwwwwww—"

"Perdu!" Scarlet shouted. "Joe! Joe—"

"Yaaaah!" That was Perdu's scream. "Scarlet! I'm dying—"

A smash, as of falling tinware. Shadows came to life, jigging in the temple entryway. A knife glinted sparks against stone, flew from the opening, bounded and rang on the gravelly steps. Echoes took up the outcry, and as Scarlet's wet hand jumped his gun from the holster a man's body lurched in the doorway, hung kicking, fighting, voicing strangled yells. Moonlight illuminated the face above the plunging body.

Perdu!

His hair blowing about his eyes, his arm waving in frantic circles in a tattered sleeve and his boots a-dance. An arm, coming from behind the door in which he was silhouetted, had him by the throat. The breath left Scarlet. A green arm. Green as grass. Muscled, thick. And Perdu couldn't shake the fingers that were trap-teeth clamped on his neck; held him jumping in the temple door. His empurpled cheeks swelled for want of breath. His eyes rolled wildly at Scarlet, imploring, white as bird's eggs, popping in his contorted face.

The Green God of Sheba!

The little curio hunter wanted to shoot that bilious green

arm jutting from behind the doorjamb, but in the uncertain moonlight he couldn't risk it. "Hang on!" he screamed at Perdu. "I'm coming!"

"Across the bridge!" Perdu managed to squall. "It's killing me!"

FOR THE life of him Peter Scarlet didn't want to rush out over that ravine. Under his boots the rope rungs sagged sickeningly. The guide-rope wobbled in his fist like a rubber band. The whole span began to creak, sway and swing like a treacherous hammock. Sweat spilled down the sides of his nose. He did not look down. He couldn't look down; couldn't take his eyes from the scene in the doorway of that old temple. Perdu had sagged to his knees, and the clutching arm was shaking him like a pump handle. He was a big man, but he couldn't fight off that green appendage. In the middle of the rope bridge Scarlet balanced frantically; shouted.

"Hold on, Perdu, I'm—"

His cry yorked out in his beard. A ripping sound under his heels. Hemp snapped beneath his feet, his legs shot through, a split-second he dangled by an elbow in midair, his knees in an empty hole pumping space, his boots fighting for a foothold in black wind. In that fractured second he had time to see two broken strands of rope sail down and down into emptiness below. In that eyewink he had time to unlimber his body for the fall. His elbow lost hold on the guide-rope, his fingers tore loose; he was falling....

The bridge made an arc above him. The moon shot like a wan scimitar thrown across the sky. Down the wind came a nail-rattle, wild inhuman laugh that might have started from the jaws of a beast. Then his boots smashed water and a geyser closed around him.

ONLY THE jack-knife twist at the start, the instinctive limbering of muscles saved him. In the smothering water he sank deep and deeper, ears roaring, lungs bursting for air. He seemed to sink a thousand fathoms while pain daggered through every bone in his frame before his boots struck mud and he swam,

half-conscious, for the surface in a black roil. Spitting, gasping
wind into exploding lungs, he floundered on the surface. The
first thing he saw was the gun still clamped in his fist. Then the
stars far above in the zenith. There was the bridge with the gap
in the middle, the hole through which he had plunged—like
a comb with the teeth missing—printed against the sky. That
wasn't all. A phantom-gray shape, a spiderish figure was swinging out across the web-thin strands.

The little curio hunter's drowned howl echoed up the sheer
glass cliffs of the ravine; but the spidery figure kept on going,
jumped the hole where the rungs were missing, reached the rim
where the motorcycle lay. A moment later Scarlet heard the
popping cylinders, the revving of the engine. Then all sound died
out. He was alone at the bottom of the world, treading water
in that well-bottom pond. Turning on his back, he shook pain
from his head and tried to think. The water was bitter salt in his
cut mouth, but the stinging stemmed blood in his nose and the
shock of the plunge was leaving him.

"Joe! Perdu! Perdu!"

The only answer was his own voice, a faint, frail, mimicry of
echoes thrown back from crags overhead. Teeth clenched in his
aching face, Scarlet turned a blinded gaze up the wall towering
over him. No fly could have climbed that sheer embankment.
The sides of this quarry might have been polished wax. Slowly he
struck for mid-pond where the ghost of the moon lay reflected
in a spectral mirror; the pool was some quarter-mile in circum-
ference and might be shallow on the other side.

The water seemed shallow in mid-pond; looked as if there
might be an island under the surface. A yellowish area underwater in moonlight. Appeared to be rising. Bubbles....

Scarlet halted his easy armstrokes, tread water, stared. An
island was rising; moving up out of the ink before his eyes. The
surface broke in a shower of bubbles and froth. The little American curio hunter started a scream that became a lump of dough

gagging his tongue. A vast, amorphous shape swelled up like a quivering nightmare in the moonlight in front of him.

Water founted.

The thing was rising like a balloon soaring from pond-bottom weeds. In the gloom a monstrous blob of faceless, living flesh reared before Scarlet's popping stare, a huge and bulbous creature: a gas bag of inflating skin—a mouth like a gigantic parrot horn—tiny, lidless eyes like twin crystals set in the puffing skin, fixing the victim with a glare of hate that brought snow on his scalp.

As Scarlet watched in frozen horror, lumps and cornices appeared, vanished, reappeared on the bulging, puffing skin. A bivalve opened under the beak-like horn with a whistling sound. The skin changed color, flashing rainbow hues, shading liver-red, lavender, pink, yellow, turning finally a poisonous mottled sea-green. Water splashed and eddied around the vast green body and in a sudden wash of foam six great, snake-thick tentacles undersurfaced with leech-pads whipped underwater and whirled around Scarlet in a spine-snapping grab.

Arms crushed to his sides, Scarlet was unable to so much as pull the gun-trigger. Those tentacles were pythons squeezing the life from his chest. Those suckers were big as lily-pads glued to his sides, drawing the strength from his body like terrible drains, dragging him under. He screamed, kicking a flurry of froth. The beast heaved; a jet of inky fluid smeared the water to a ghastly roil. Quickly, sinewed with gigantic submarine strength, the octopus yanked Scarlet through the water with a succession of convulsive jerks.

The little curio hunter's veins flowed ice. Fighting with every ounce of power in his lamed frame, he battled to break the grip of those terrible, boneless arms that held him fast. Another tentacle, secreted underwater, slipped about his ankles. He broke the hold with a desperate kick; found his boots ploughing in mud.

In the shallows of that forgotten quarry pond overshadowed

by a temple ancient as Solomon's glory, man and sea monster thrashed the water to fountains.

SICK, HORROR-FROZEN, helpless in the suction-grip of the giant tentacles, Scarlet was dragged into the shadow of the precipice, toward a cavernous undercut where the cliff was scalloped out like a mammoth clamshell; a recess filled with weedy moonlight. Sea snails and salt crystals jeweled the scooped walls, water gurgled from crevices in the stone; here the octopus lay in its marine lair, a horrid, convulsing emerald in a Tiffany setting.

Two ghastly legs slithered like cobras up the wall to moor the creature in its cave like a dreadful fleshy parasite growing there; the body filled the cavern; the six free legs bound Scarlet in a clutch as foul as the suck of quicksand. Bound in a cocoon of gluey muscles, he was yanked, kicking, across the shallow ledge; drawn inch by inch toward the billowing, shapeless mound of body, toward the lid-less stare of those salt-crusted eyes, toward that horn-like mouth.

He shrieked, but no sound issued from his lips. He struggled, stamping, flailing his boots. The contracting muscle-fish arms drew him nearer and nearer to the awful embrace. On the ledge the water lay scarcely two feet deep. The little curio hunter was being landed like a fish yanked ashore by six lines.

The lines played with him, tossed him against the wall. Battered, suffocating, he smashed a kick at the gas-bag body— like sinking his boot in a pillow. Air soughed from the valve in the monster's side. Air whistled from Scarlet's pinched windpipe. A contortion of rage quivered through the sea giant's body, swelling its mass like a frog-belly to the bursting point. The shallows plunged, waved to a tiny tempest. Water spurted and founted at Scarlet's face. Sand and sea shells whirled around his head. The little cavern shivered with windy sounds. The beast was drowning him, banging him at the wall, crushing him, killing him. He was fainting.

In a last desperate explosion of energy, Scarlet pounded the sand with his boots, twisting, writhing, battling to get away. On his knees, kicking. Foam flying around his head. Boots punching and stabbing while the arms that held him shook him like a rat. Weeds and starfish, brought up from the bottom, whirled by his face. And something else, thrown to the surface by the whirlpool. Something that knotted Scarlet's throat in his neck and brought a yell from his slashed mouth.

A man's sun helmet!

A man's sun helmet, waterlogged and half filled with sand, bobbed past his eyes like an old bucket and sailed out to mid-pond. An empty coat came up on the whirl and floated out of the cave, the vacant sleeves bobbing outstretched on the foaming water. And then, to wrench the last cry from the curio hunter's throat, a muddy black bag ducked by his head. A doctor's medicine case, soggy and battered, spinning around him in the foam.

Peter Scarlet recognized that doctor's kit. Not an inch from his chin the case floated, bobbed, sank again. Scarlet lashed out a kick and his flying boot struck the bag squarely on the handle, sent it whirling through froth straight at the sea monster's little eyes. Rotten leather burst to shreds.

And then the miracle happened.

A SHOWER of bottles scattered in the gloom, smashing in bright explosions of glass against the cavern wall. Pill boxes and packets and glass jars smashed in tiny shrapnel burst against wet stone. A rain of colored liquids, a shower of pills and powder filled the moonlight.

A streak of amber liquor and broken glass rippled between the staring sea devil's eyes. Where the pills struck, water bubbles rose. The water seemed to boil, steaming and hissing, a witch's cauldron. A film of smoke choked Scarlet's lungs. A smell of burning acids, raw poisons, seared flesh. The octopus writhed, flailed, contorted to a thousand shapes; yanked its mooring tentacles from the wall and lashed the water to a frenzy.

The arms about Scarlet uncoiled like agonized whips; flinging him headlong from the shallow ledge.

If he lived to be a million he would never forget the sight of that monstrous beast puffing and swelling, whirling and deflating and hurling its bulk from side to side, its eight arms slashing air, water and walls like a hundred maddened pythons in a jar of chemicals. Blinded, burned, the monster raised a storm that lashed the whole pond with tidal waves. The little American curio hunter made the fastest swim of his life to mid-pool where an empty coat floated on the surface, its sleeves outspread. Through a mist of pain he snatched the garment in a white-fingered clasp; remembered the Webley automatic fastened in his fist; turned and fired twice at the thing in the cavern. Treading water, he waited, gasping, until silence filled the cave.... Until the waters were black and still, a shadow bulged on the shelf like a rock and only a faint, acidulous steam wafted from the glooms.

"Doc!" he whispered.

Stroking slowly with bruised arms, he made for the shallows, stood up, dripping like a weed, and turned his face to the sky. Rage and relief that shivered through him seemed to clear his mind. Leveling the automatic in his palm, he emptied bullets at the stars. On that side of the ravine where the temple loomed, ropes parted at their mooring posts. The bridge of hemp soared down like a broken hammock and hung, a shaky Jacob's ladder, on the south wall. The bottom rungs just reached the water.

To the little curio hunter it seemed hours before he had scaled that precipice, dragged his boots at last from the maw of that quarried ravine. On the way up, where the rungs were missing, he'd lost hold, almost fallen. Snatching to keep his grip on the coat he'd found, he came within an ace of dropping. It was then he saw the bit of soggy notepaper in the coat pocket.

When he got to the top where the horses were tethered, he knelt on the ground and spread the sopping paper across his knee and read the penciled message with his face going to chalk in the moonlight. He didn't look back at the ravine. He drew one breath through his teeth and made a lunge for the nearest mount. Africa made black wind through his hair, and the moon was a red sickle sinking in the heart of the sky.

CHAPTER VI

THE *Red Sea Lady's* quartermaster, who saw Peter Scarlet walk up the gangway and stumble to his corridor, shouted to the engineer at the rail alongside. "I guess that ain't the first passenger to come back aboard drunk an' beat up. Must of got rolled in some joint ashore. I told him not to walk in Terbera alone at night."

The Scotch engineer grunted. "Fools who go ashore an' spend all their money in dives. Huh. By Gord, I wish they'd finish unloadin' them rails. Th' noise will deef me. We sails in an hour, you say?"

It was, by the cracked dial of Peter Scarlet's wrist watch, four o'clock. In his stateroom he bathed, combed, jabbed adhesive plaster to one corner of his mouth, drank two glasses straight. The crash of falling iron shook the porthole frame. Africa's smells and yells trampled around the ship, and the little American curio hunter smiled bleakly in approval, servicing his Webley automatic. You saw by the way he punched in fresh shells and snapped the clip he was not unfamiliar with guns. Then he pulled a sun helmet over his welted forehead, left his stateroom and turned for Cabin A.

Only one witness saw him walk into Cabin A without knocking: the man at the washstand inside. This man turned with soap bubbles on his arm, and Scarlet closed the door swiftly behind him.

The little American curio hunter took a cigarette from his beard, pinched it out in his fingers, dropped it on the floor and ground it underheel. It was hot in that stateroom. Suffocating. Perspiration ran in freshets down the face of the man at the washstand where he stood stiff as a plank, pop-eyed with fright, his mouth framing a soundless *O.* But Peter Scarlet's face was dry. So was his voice. Dry as sand grinding between stones.

"I might have known," he said evenly, "when I found my room wasn't paid for at Rhodesian Willy's. Tight-fisted dealing. Miser complex. A rat who'd murder his own mother to keep from sharing anything with her. It's all over now. No more of that. I stopped at the Spaniard's on th' way back an' put a gun in his belly an' he told me where you were. First boat out you could get, of course."

"No! No, no, no!" the man whispered. "Wha—whaaaa—"

"I knew I was up against a scrooging rat who'd want to keep everything for himself. I was the only other one in on the big secret I knew about the find. Idea was to get me down here and ambush me. Minute I step ashore I'm attacked. The knifer misses the mark so I'm planted in a hotel room to be a target for hired gunmen waiting across the street. The sniper gets sniped on the job and his henchmen get you word, and I'm led to the slaughter on that sea road to Ras Harar. And when *those* jackals fail to stop me at the lighthouse, why there's the rope bridge with the rungs sawed in the middle—"

"My God! You got me wrong. You don't believe Joe Perdu would—you don't think old Joe could be—"

"A pretty trap," Scarlet's words ground on relentlessly. "I'd fall down that ravine into the quarry pool. If I didn't break my neck, the octopus would get me anyway. How long do you suppose that rotten sea monster has been living in that pond? Maybe put there by the ancient priests, eh? Put there to play Green God of Sheba for tribal rituals. Nice way to sacrifice a victim," Scarlet snarled, "just as Doc was sacrificed. He fell through the bridge same as me and that filthy death got him. Yeah. I found his helmet, coat and—and medicine case in that monster's cave. Let me read you the note I found in his coat pocket—"

The man had to grip the washstand to support his legs. His lips were the color of grass on the cry: "Please! God's sake—"

"Here it is," Scarlet gritted. "It says: *'Doc: Come back to camp. Bring medicine and hurry. I'm dying of fever. Don't fail me.'* He must have been in Terbera waiting to catch the mail boat when he got this dirty message—"

"Help!" the green lips screamed. "Stewards! Save me—"

"And Doc hurried back to that rotten camp and the—the octopus got him. But he left a little boomerang in that trap, you rat. His medicine case. Ha! There were poisons in that kit. He always carried vitriol. And hydrofluoric acid. Enough to blind that devil fish—"

"Stewards! Help! In the name of—"

The voice rose to shrill crescendo.

"Go ahead, scream," Scarlet was shouting. "Scream like you did in the door of that temple, with your own filthy arm coming from behind the door pretending to strangle you. Just washing off the green ink, aren't you? Or maybe that's the color of your soul coming through, I've seen that trick before, but I— Scream. Sure. All you want. Look at this gun. *Look* at it, Joe Perdu. Remember, I'm a sharpshooter. And scream your face off. They won't hear the shot. They say the noise out on that pier would wake the dead. Well, here's one dead man it won't!"

> There Were Two On That Ship Down The African Seas—
> When The Watch Went To Ring One Bell—
> And One Man's Ticket Read Home—
> And One Man's Ticket Read Hell—

BLOOD OF THE BEAST

*Out of the green choking jungles of the East crept
a renegade pair—a man and a beast trailing
a kill-command. And a little Yankee curio-
hunter was bait for their maniac dead-fall.*

A WESTERING SUN was dropping behind black jungle when Peter Scarlet, the little American curio-hunter, reached his bungalow. Twilight lay death-quiet over the dark verandah, and the afterglow spread a ghostly pallor in the patch of sandalwood before the door. From the mud of the sluggish river a wispy wind blew, dank and fetid.

Peter Scarlet swabbed at his forehead and mumbled a curse in his beard.

"Damn you, Bradshaw," he muttered.

He was feverish, hungry, fatigued. His journey into Minang was about to show results when Bradshaw's roundabout message came. He was hot on the trail of a carved emerald he long had wanted when a flat-nosed native plundered in, relaying Bradshaw's come-ye.

"Meet you at your place soon as possible," Scarlet scoffed. He spat irritably. "Utmost importance."

His ride under a staggering copper sky had baked the eyes in his head, and the breathless, steamy jungle before that had almost exhausted his reserve energy. He slid wearily from the native pony and left the animal wandering to its stable. His legs were weak as he walked, and he staggered a little. That meant quinine. Quickly, and in strong doses. He went on slowly across the clearing.

"Where in hell is that fool boy of mine?" he fretted as his *kit-mut-gar* failed to appear. "First Bradshaw. Then my coolies fall behind and get mired up for a week. And now my house servant sleeps on his job! What a hell of a country!"

On the verandah he dropped his provision-box, and directed a few of those good round oaths of the sea at the boy whom he guessed to be dozing inside.

Hoping to catch the boy loafing, Scarlet tiptoed to the door and gently pushed it open. As he did so, night drank up the last filtering ray of twilight in a gulp, and flung a burden of darkness over the jungle. Thick darkness. The kind of blackness that can be grabbed between the fingers. It was so sudden and so Stygian and so infernally hushed that it made the little American curio-hunter mighty nervous. He did not enjoy that jungle night.

Nerves tingling, he peered into the silent bungalow. An oath dropped from his lips. The hair rose on the nape of his neck. Gooseflesh quivered on his spine. Staring from the murk that marked the center of the room was a tiny red eye. Biting through the inky gloom it glared like a blood ruby, a single coal of fire.

Peter Scarlet, recovered from the shock, laughed. "Wow! but that's spooky! That cigaret burns like a demon's eye. Bradshaw, you give a fellow the chills. Why do you sit smoking in this damned dark room?"

But it was not Bradshaw. It was not the hard-bitten animal-hunter who was Peter Scarlet's friend. The tone of voice that answered almost threw Scarlet from his feet. It was a hoarse-slovenly, sneering tone, with a peculiar tongue-tied qual-ity—the angering, domineering drawl of a swashbuckling bully.

Scarlet did not recognize the voice, but he had heard the tone a thousand times. The Port Said sailor who had filched his luggage owned such a voice. So did the rascally skipper on the wallowing bumboat that raided the river ports.

The voice snarled, "Come in, mister. Make yerself to home."

Peter Scarlet would have given his Providence bank account right then to have had his gun. He would have given his price-less collection of rare Brahman jewelry. But his weapons were on his horse, and his horse was in the stable.

"Who's that?" he demanded, his voice husky with anger. "Who the devil are you? You sure have rare crust being in my bungalow! Get that? *My* bungalow!"

"So?" leered the voice. The cigaret described a series of arcs in the blackness. "You're Scarlet, eh? Well, come on in, Scarlet. I'll tell you now there's a gun pointing at your belly, and it don't miss often. Come in. Sit down. I'll introduce myself."

Flaring suddenly, a match lit up the room. Peter Scarlet was a sick man then; almost fainted from nausea. The flickering flame illuminated a countenance too hideous for conception—eyes like blinking black buttons sewed on a sheet of mottled canvas, eyebrows almost meeting hair, scrubby brown bush straggling over gaunt cheeks to bovine jaw. But what caused the mist of horror to clamp on Scarlet's eyelids was the terrible expression lent the visage by a torturous, burning scar that streaked like a hot wire from under the right eye, smack across the lips to the left side of the drooping chin.

The horrible face laughed.

"That's why I sit in the dark, Scarlet," the slurred voice said. "I like the dark, Scarlet, ever since your friend Bradshaw did this to me."

The match glimmered out. The little American, paralyzed with dread, shrank in the darkness. Another match spluttered, and he was in hell again.

That devil-face—

That mad, Satanic laughter.…

"My name is Gans," the scarred horror said. "Tiger Gans they used to call me." He lit a candle on the table, and Peter Scarlet saw the pair of ponderous British Army automatics that were lying there. "I worked with Bradshaw once—"

And then Peter Scarlet remembered. Half-forgotten words whirled in his brain and turned his blood to ice. Tiger Gans— the ape-man! Gans—the Khaboul killer! Peter Scarlet's knees began to tremble. Bradshaw had mumbled the tale to him long ago. Bradshaw's face was battered when he told it, and the marks of human claws were still ripped on his chest. He told Peter Scarlet of his assistant who had suddenly gone mad. How the man had howled like a beast, killed a native, attacked his own wife; of his wild fury when Bradshaw intervened. Bradshaw had been armed only with a quirt, and had been compelled to beat the maniac into bloody senselessness to save his own skin. Gans was the name of the killer, Scarlet remembered now. He had been sent to the island prison for the criminally insane.

Peter Scarlet's beard was wet with perspiration.

"You remember, eh?" the scarred killer drooled. "Yes, I see you remember. But that was ten years ago. Bradshaw beat me then. He stole my wife and he sent me to hell. Said the blood of the beast was in me.... Yes, Bradshaw held all the cards then, but now it's my turn. Now the winning hand is mine...."

His laugh rasped in the hell-hot room.

He touched the ponderous automatics. "These," he croaked, "are aces." He lifted two massive, hairy, stub-fingered hands and clenched them in the candle-light.

"These are the other two.... Four aces.... And here's the card that tops the deck—that takes all tricks—"

Reaching under his chair he found a heavy cord. With a merciless yank he jerked the rope, and from under the table came a savage screech. The next minute another devil ruled hell—the very brother of the corpse-faced Dick Gans; the only creature on earth to share his throne with him.

"Meet Joker," announced the scarred atrocity. "The damndest and wickedest and strongest orang-outang going!"

PETER SCARLET, the American curio-hunter, had attained the distinction of fifty years at the time of this story. Twenty of those years he had devoted to the Orient with a passion that grew as each sunset painted the sky; and he was no novice in the strange and extraordinary adventures that the East might stage.

A score of terrifying experiences had found him cast in the leading role. He had, with fierce energy, once resisted the damning anguish of a Chinese water-torture. He had survived the

horror of being flung into the Ganges amidst a battling mess
of foul fanatics—that water just writhed with disease. He had
crawled, thirsting, across a frying desert waste, and had spent
a screaming afternoon in a Siam jungle at grips with a python
as relentless as flying hours to an aged man, as strong as twenty
oxen. Small wonder that his hair—little enough on his head but
plenty on his chin—had blown a trifle snowy. Yet he remained
adamant to the beseeching letters from old friends.

"Come back," they cried, "to America. You old fool, stop this
silly traipsing over Asia after bric-a-brac. Why don't you live
like a human being? Come back to New York—"

And the little man's sea-blue eyes would twinkle, his bronze
cheeks and forehead would wrinkle up in a grin; for paralleling
his volcano temper was an equally violent sense of humor.

"Like a human being—" he would laugh. "In New York!"

But he was sorely tempted to return after that ghastly ordeal
in the nerve-shattering company of Tiger Gans, his four aces,
and the trick-taking top card, the orang-outang, Joker.

Just a glimpse of Gans was enough to appall any man, and his
ape was little better; a mangy, offensive, sullen brute with steel
muscles and saw-like fangs.

"I broke away six weeks ago," Gans said in his crazy, lisping
voice. "We are tired. We will rest here. In a few days my message
will bring Bradshaw running, just as my other message brought
you. Maybe he'll steal my new wife"—he jerked on the ape's
chain and laughed as the beast screamed—"like he stole my
other one."

Peter Scarlet tried to speak but his voice was a burnt whisper.
What use to explain that the woman had died long since from
the fury of Gans' own hairy fists?

"We'll wait for him," Tiger Gans rasped. "The three of us. It's
a nice quiet place for what I'll do to Bradshaw." And suddenly
the barrel of his right-hand automatic was pointing at Scarlet's belly. "Sit down, Shorty. Take a chair, Old Whiskers, and

listen close. Do what I say and you live. Make a move that I don't like—"

He snarled deep in his throat.

Tiger Gans. A tiger snarling—

He said, "Joker and I understand each other, see, Old Whiskers? If you find a knife and stab me while I sleep, Joker will fix you. You wouldn't let him harm me, would you, Joker, my little companion?"

He accompanied the question with a kick that hurled the ape against the wall. The beast screeched curses at its master, but the fear of God was in its red-rimmed eye.

"See, Old Whiskers?" He smiled as only such a face could smile. "Joker understands. He's almost as afraid of me as you are. He hates me almost as much. But he knows I can handle him. He obeys. Just like you'll obey—"

He was rising as he spoke, enormously tall, and like a jungle cat he came around the table. His long arm shot out, paw open, and crashed against Peter Scarlet's face. The little American curio-hunter spun across the room and slumped against the wall. While he lay there, weak and furious, the madman began to prove his marksmanship by driving bullets into a few of Scarlet's cherished curios.

Scarlet writhed and spluttered in an agony of dread. The ape jabbered and mimicked him from its retreat in a corner. And Tiger Gans bellowed with hollow, evil laughter.

"Tiffin!" he roared then. "Jump some food on the table, Old Whiskers."

SO BEGAN three days of exquisite torture for Peter Scarlet. He found the prostrate form of his *kit-mut-gar* bent double beside the camp stove. Joker had playfully done that, Tiger Gans told Scarlet between bites of the *chippatis* that the curio-hunter had been forced to offer. It was also suggested that one false step on Scarlet's part, and Joker might toy with Scarlet.

Speechless and horrified, Peter Scarlet watched the boy's body dragged from the bungalow and tossed into the green river. Rose a flurried commotion of splashing water and flipping tails. Mud moved.

"Trot out some rum, Old Whiskers!"

Raging, the little curio-hunter did as he was ordered; praying only for the intervention of a visitor, or the chance to find a weapon. But the rack of rifles that had been in the gun-room had disappeared, and his every move was watched. Joker shambled around at his heels through the rooms, grinning, stinking fiend with powerful hands that Scarlet knew could crush him as if he were a bird's egg. The madman had fastened shut all the blinds and kept the door closed. Scarlet had not the slightest chance of bolting.

In two hours the bungalow had been reduced to a shambles. Gans flung himself all over the place, wantonly smashing things up, and occasionally hurling boots and crockery at Joker. The ape thoroughly enjoyed the fun, and twirled back any missile that came to hand, until a monsoon might have been blowing over the American's place.

Like a barroom wench Scarlet slaved and cooked and fed his two captors, wading miserably about in a heap of trash, watching apprehensively as the ape, in devilish enjoyment, wandered from one infamy to another, tearing down tapestries, smashing dishware, and spilling wreckage over everything.

Tiger Gans sat back and spoke in ugly, lisping detail of the things he would do to Bradshaw when the animal-man arrived. Peter Scarlet was scared sick of him, and he knew it. He knew that the little man was going mad with horror of him, and was well pleased.

"But wait till Bradshaw comes!" he would say, and laugh his awful mirth again.

Scarlet would have thrown himself at his tormentor, unequal as that fight would have been, had not it meant certain death at the hands of the orang-outang. Scarlet ached with the hate of him. He lay awake all night wildly planning escape, tortured by the memory of his captor's countenance, shivering at the ghastly snores that whistled from the mutilated face.

Peter Scarlet stayed awake. And the orang-outang stayed awake and watched Peter Scarlet. Tiger Gans kept a weather eye out for the orang-outang and Peter Scarlet.

Scarlet would move. The ape would move. Tiger Gans would move.

Outside the black jungle steamed, weltering under tropic night, throbbing with the stillness of the catacombs.

PETER SCARLET awoke from a stupor-like doze into living nightmare. Shrill cries were issuing from the verandah which was flooded crimson under boiling, morning sunglow. Gans was beating his ape. It was not nice. The animal screams were almost human.

Scarlet could have yelled in frenzy. He scrambled from the chair in which he had spent the night, and groaned with a thousand sore muscles. As he gained his feet the screaming ape fled into the room and bounded under the table, where it crouched, quivering with fear.

Tiger Gans followed. His face was livid, and Scarlet moaned as he saw it. That was not a face. The knobby forehead was boiling with purple veins, and cheeks flushed with drink. The scar disfiguring the mouth was dyed violet.

"Good God!" Scarlet could not restrain the cry.

The madman whirled on the American. A razor-strap dangled in his hairy fist. With a grunt he drove the leather strap about Scarlet's legs, and Scarlet bawled with pain. *Slash!* It was a barbarous blow, and the little curio-hunter hopped under the smart of it. A cutting lash. It drove terror into Scarlet's heart as it had driven terror into the ape's. But it drove an idea into his mind. That cut from the brutal razor-strap drove an idea into Scarlet's chaotic mind.

Gans stood glaring at him from savage eyes.

"You fool!" he snarled. "Shall I give you both a lesson? Bradshaw will be here late tomorrow, but there's time to tame you both again if needed. Joker bit at me this morning. He hates me as you do. But I'll blaze the fear—"

Peter Scarlet made no sound. He was fondling his idea. He knew that when Bradshaw came the big animal-hunter would be easy meat for the madman's trap. Unprepared—unwatchful. There were two lives wavering in the balance.

The snarl died in Tiger Gans' throat. He cuffed Scarlet's face with the back of his hand. "Keep your tongue still, Old Whiskers. Now serve out more rations."

He cracked the heavy strap.

"Joker!"

The brute sidled out from under the table, to squat before its master. It chewed aimlessly on a crust, thumped the floor with its knuckles, and chattered peevishly.

Peter Scarlet knew, and the maniac Gans knew that the ape wanted nothing more than to sink its fangs into the Tiger's imbecile forehead. And that ape knew it, too. It wanted nothing more in all the world than to destroy this monster of a man who had tamed and tortured it. But Joker's animal heart had been beaten to mash, crushed to submission. The ape dared not resist; dared only to serve.

The razor-strap flicked before Joker's eyes. "See this! You get it every time you show your teeth at me!" He gestured to Scarlet. "Come on, Whiskers. Lively with the provender."

Boiling with resentment, Scarlet obeyed. He dared not resist. Not yet. So he brought his captor cold *chippatis,* hot tea, and despite his filthy surroundings, managed to eat something, himself. Later in the morning he contrived to sneak down a stiff nobbler of gin, and felt considerably braced.

Not once that day did the little curio-hunter get out of his captor's sight. But he was growing accustomed to Gans' shocking visage, and learned to avoid the ape. He realized that as long as he made no hostile move toward Gans he was safe from the brute. So he held himself in to play a waiting game.

The bungalow was reduced to complete wreckage that morning by Joker's vagaries.

Peter Scarlet spent the afternoon on the floor playing at dice with his captor. Tiger Gans made him play. He forced the game with the two British Army automatics, and much hardy profanity. Sweating, Scarlet rolled the dice, and tried to concentrate on his plan.

Gans pulled steadily on a gin bottle. Joker sniffed about the room, examining and smashing articles with monotonous regularity.

Scarlet strove in desperation to think clearly. He must concentrate! But it is difficult to concentrate when one is feverish, squats on the floor in a heap of trash with an ugly orang-outang at one elbow, and two husky automatics at the other—automatics wielded by a creature whose face was simply monstrous in the dim light. And Tiger Gans was fondling those army guns all the time. Was he tiring of his game? Would he wait until Bradshaw arrived before killing Peter Scarlet?

A SCALDING yellow moon sailed over the black patch of sandalwood that night, and Peter Scarlet, lying awake watching it through the blinds, wondered if he would ever see it again. Beside him, on a heap of blankets, Tiger Gans snored in animal slumber. Animal slumber—for if Scarlet stirred uneasily one of the madman's eyes would pop open and stare like a shark's eye in the moonlight. Scarlet could see it. The ape was always sighing, and scraping about.

Peter Scarlet was deathly afraid of that beast. He had seen the remains of a naturalist who had ventured argument with an angry orang-outang. There had been difficulty in identifying those remains. Perspiring from every pore, Scarlet fought to control his nerves and lie quiet on the floor. Lying there in the moonlight, listening to his captor's wailing snores and the alert movements of the ape, Scarlet watched the yellow moon rise into the mysterious jungle night sky; and he planned. He planned on the idea suggested by the razor-strapping he had received that morning.

The ape watched him, but could not read his mind.

When the plan had been formulated, Scarlet settled down to pray. Few men could pray as fervently as that little curio-hunter did that night. He prayed with all his heart. With all his soul. Sweat formed on his whispering lips.

The sandalwoods murmured accompaniment, and heavy scents from distant jungle land drifted through the blinds....

Peter awoke with a terrified start, horrified that he had slept. Snores at his side, ghostly snores, told him that his captor was still there. With an effort, Scarlet sat up. Came a snarl. The ape watched him with guttural growls. Gans blinked awake, thumbed his eyes, and yawned. The game was on.

A well-aimed gin bottle sent Joker screaming under the table. Scarlet was glad, seeing the hate sparkle from the ape's eyes.

Gans turned toward him, his button eyes glistening in the horrid mask of his face. "Today's the day, Old Whiskers," said his dreadful lisp. "First you'll straighten up the place here. Make everything usual. When Bradshaw comes in sight you'll do as I tell you." He chuckled. "How about some food, Old Whiskers?"

Scarlet licked his lips, nodded.

A snarl of command brought the ape crawling from under the table. Gans cursed him, taunted him, and when Joker showed his fangs struck viciously with the barrel of his Army automatic. The ape screamed like a woman, vanished in a corner.

"Food, Old Whiskers!" Tiger Gans bellowed.

Every minute Peter Scarlet spent cooking over the camp stove, he would have traded a fortune for an ounce of poison. The cool of dawn was still in the air, but sweat streamed down his cheeks. He staggered a little as he carried in the rice cakes; leaned weakly against the wall as Gans wolfed them down.

"A drink—" Gans shouted.

Scarlet darted into the gun room. It was a room that had been the pride of his heart. Now prize pelts, photographs, hunting jackets, helmets, lay in confusion on the floor.

"May that ape squirm in hell for a million years!"

In a corner he located a case of brandy, and grabbed up a bottle. The drunker Gans was, the better.

"Lively there—" Gans called after him.

Scarlet sprang to an overturned traveling kit. It was a dusty old-kit filled with junk; had been in the bungalow for years. Nervous fingers flew into the bag, and with a "Thank God!" Scarlet found what he wanted. He found what had been suggested by that razor-strap. An old-fashioned, rusty instrument, relic of Scarlet's youth when his beard had not been—a nickel-plated straight-edge razor. With quivering fingers he hid it in his shirt and hurried to pour the maniac's drink.

When Gans staggered from his breakfast to the verandah, Peter Scarlet could have whooped with joy. Wildly excited, he began brushing away the dirty, broken crockery, and picking up the myriad articles that the ape had strewn over the room. As he neared the table he fairly shook with anxiety.

The ape watched him from the doorway. Turning his back to the animal, he drew the razor from his shirt, opened the blade, and slid it under the table. It was an extremely long chance—a desperate chance. But Peter Scarlet knew that nothing but an extremely long chance could save him.

WHEN TIGER Gans came inside and closed the door Scarlet was fussing over the camp stove. The ape was picking over a heap of shattered crockery.

"Joker!" growled its master.

The beast looked up fearfully.

Tiger Gans snatched up a chair leg, and advanced toward the ape. Gans was just having fun. He chuckled. He loved to terrify the animal and see it cringe before him. It was good discipline. Scarlet was almost exploding with nerves. Gans might have noticed his captive fidgeting about, but most people fidgeted when he was near, and he did not notice.

"Joker," he crooned, and whirled the chair leg.

The ape ducked under the table.

Peter Scarlet was almost fainting with agitation. The whole affair played into his scheme. He had noted that every time its master abused it the ape retreated under the table. Thus the plan. The razor-strap had recalled to Scarlet his unused blade. At first he had been tempted to attack his captor, or cut the fiend's throat as he slept. But that meant subsequent battle with Joker, the ape, and Scarlet dared not chance the encounter, for he was a little fellow of slight build, and the ape could have crackled him to jelly despite the razor.

The ape would not let Scarlet approach the maniac, but if Gans should chance to torment it, might not the ape itself attack its cruel master, given an advantage? Scarlet had put the razor within the beast's reach, and now he waited. The animal might do any of a hundred things, or nothing. It might cut its own throat. Scarlet almost wished it would. Or it might battle its tormentor.

Petrified with expectancy, Peter Scarlet watched.

Jabbering under the table, Joker spied the shiny blade, and almost cut a hand apart in clutching at it.

It is doubtful what the outcome would have been had not Tiger Gans tried to settle it.

The ape danced from its retreat, playfully flourishing the bright blade, jibbering with pleasure. Gans saw the razor, and yelled. The ape waved the instrument. The madman fought to draw his guns, and backing away, aimed a kick at the brute. For the first time the ape saw fear in its master's eye. Yes, the ape saw fear, and recognized it!

Pent up hate welled into the savage breast. With a murderous snarl it flew straight at Tiger Gans, landed on his chest, and swept out with the razor, carving a large portion of scalp from the killer's skull.

Blood pouring into his eyes, Gans fell shrieking and fighting to the floor. When Joker saw that blood he jerked a scream into space that rang in the jungle like a siren—an exultant, fierce cry.

Scarlet had rushed into the gun room, battered out a blind, dived from the bungalow, and raced to hide in the stable. He had hoped to find his carbine and saddle-pistols, but the pony had wandered away. Pale, crouching in the straw, he listened to the crash and cry of combat.

Followed silence. Silence in the bungalow.

Tense with caution, Scarlet crept to peer from the stable door.

He was just in time to see Joker, the ape, fiendishly jabbering, drag a limp, silent, sagging burden from the open gun room casement, and lug it off among the sandalwood trees.

That was the last thing Peter Scarlet saw. His fevered, tortured mind went blank then, and his body wilted. When next he opened his eyes he was staring at a sunset sky. Bradshaw was lifting him, calling his name, cursing.

PETER SCARLET, the little American curio-hunter, does not play cards any more. To those who knew him when he loved nothing better than to shirt-sleeve a night away hard at a furiously contested poker game his new attitude is decidedly mysterious. Now he never so much as glances at a deck of playing cards.

And you could not induce him to go back into that jungle south of Minang. Peter Scarlet would not have returned to that jungle for anything, despite his passion for curios. He would not have gone back into that jungle for the pelt of Buddah's tiger, or the whispering rubies of Jehan Jee—no—nor the fabled beard of Mohammed! And those *are* inducements.

THE EVIL EYE

There is more than one man in the East who would pay a handsome price for Peter Scarlet's head on a platter. Scarlet knows this fact—and laughs at his enemies. But he did not laugh when Ludwig Von Groot's dead finger pointed a path he must follow.

THIS IS THE story of a dead man's eyes and how he kept them alive to aim the gun of a dead man.

It happened down there in the Moluccas where you spit one way toward Celebes and curse the other toward Guinea; and where God, they say, keeps His back turned; but the man who turned *his* back would get a knife in it.

The dead man was buried in far-off Java, but his eyes went on living on that Molucca island in a dark stone castle built on sin. A Portuguese pirate mixed the *castillo* cement with blood, and a Chinese admiral had plastered the turrets with the bones of slaves. Years later Spain had used it for a pest house, and the Black Hole of Calcutta was a wishing well compared to the dungeons underneath.

The gray walls scowled against a sky like heated brass; the towers overlooked a jungle where headhunters scrawled to their smoke-fests, and crocodiles snoozed in warm mud. Now the headhunters were gone and the pirates were gone; and the last man to live there—Herr Ludwig Von Groot—was dead and buried in a distant grave.

But the evil that men do lives after them. The next five visitors to that island castle never came out alive.

This is what happened to the sixth—

CHAPTER I

PETER SCARLET, THE little American curio-hunter, listened to the British policeman's story, and at the end he asked two questions.

"You say this Von Groot was a gunsmith before he came to the Orient? A gun-smith in Berlin?"

"That's right," the officer panted.

"And how long does it take to get to that island from Ternate?"

"About four hours, I should guess. There's a dirty little trading schooner run by a Frenchman."

Scarlet poured a whisky through his short-chopped beard. He pushed back his chair, and picked his automatic from the veranda wall. "Thanks for the dope, Captain. I'm going"

"But, good God!" the Englishman cried. "You know what happened to those others. Five of them. And there isn't a trace, I tell you! You *can't* go down there alone."

"I'm going," Scarlet nodded, "and I've got just the man to go along." Leaving the consulate, he cut across the shimmering market place to the telegraph office, and scribbled a hurry-call:

> Meet me in Ternate soon as possible. Want you look at valuable masterpiece.

All in all, the whole thing was queer. Wilhelm Schneider, the beery Dutch artist from Islamahad, came panting and sweating on the first mail ship south, and met the little American curio-hunter on the Ternate dock. Without giving the Dutchman a chance to draw his breath, Scarlet hurried him aboard the schooner. Afternoon was waning as the craft heeled down the Molucca Sea, and the curio-hunter hustled his friend into a stuffy cabin.

For half an hour Scarlet chatted of old times, uncorking drinks. Islands slid by, green and purple in the yellow heat. Ragged, rice-white beaches and jungly shorelines where tropic vegetation tumbled down steep cliffs into narrow lagoons. There was a smell of decay in the afternoon, but no air. The schooner shuffled down the archipelago, its sails pushed by the smell. The cabin was like a stove, and the Dutchman's pores began to melt. It was too much like an excursion. All too calm. Schneider didn't like it. He had seen that look on the little curio-hunter's face before.

The skipper, a six-foot Frenchman out of Port Macquarie with a face as mean and lumpy as a piece of peanut-brittle, went catfooting by the door. His glance swivelled sidewise as he passed, and Scarlet shut the door with a kick. Then the little American leaned across the table and fastened a grip on the Dutchman's arm.

"Frenchy's gone aft to the wheel—now we can talk. That Frog claims he can't speak English, but we're taking no chances. Listen, Wilhelm, did you ever hear of a German named Ludwig Von Groot?"

Schneider mopped stickiness from his temples and shook his head. Mynheer Schneider was a fat man, and fat men don't like mysteries. Mynheer Schneider liked kegs of beer and tubs of good food and time to paint pictures in oil colors.

"*In Gottes Namen* what is that all about, Peter? You wire me to meet you and look at a valuable work of art. Then you get me on this *verdammt* schooner sailing down the middle of Nowhere. You are on pins and needles. What is it about?"

"It's about this German, Ludwig Von Groot," the little curio-hunter said softly. "Yes, and there's a picture in it, too—we're coming to that." He poured fresh fingers of whisky; sent a quick

gaze out of the porthole where bugs and heat glimmered against the glass. "Did you ever hear of that old Portuguese castle in the islands down here?"

"*Ja,*" the Dutchman grunted, "I haff heard of such a place."

"That's where we're going," Scarlet growled, "because there's hell to pay and I'd like you in at the pay-off. But I'll hand you the yarn and if you don't want it you can go back."

Wilhelm Schneider sopped at a worried face. "I don't want it already, but I'll stick. Who was Ludwig Von Groot?"

The little curio-hunter cleared his throat with an oath. "He's the baby who last owned this Portuguese castle. Von Groot came to the Dutch East Indies some time around 1910. Far as I can learn he was once a gun-smith in Berlin. Then he cut his trail out here and started a land-office business in piracy and murder. He was a killer, I can tell you, and guns had always been his specialty. Crack-shot with a pistol and would have shot his own mother to sell her hair. Anyway he set up headquarters in this island castle and played hell from Port Moresby to Singapore."

The cabin swayed gently, and the curio-hunter's voice swam at Schneider through the heat: "By 1913 Von Groot was feared from China to Port Said. Nobody dared touch him, and he'd

collared himself a fortune and ran this island like a king. Then he showed up in Penang on an opium job and shot a young lad named Grover dead on the street.... This kid was a friend of mine," Scarlet whispered, "and I swore I'd get Von Groot if it was the last thing I did. Young Grover had a lot of good friends. I collected a bunch of them, and we started out to nail Von Groot. There were five besides myself. A naturalist named John McCord. Mallison, the engineer from the cinnabar mines where Grover worked. An Italian big-game hunter named Giavetti. Captain Charlie Loo of the China Coast trade. And a lad from the British consulate named Dree."

Something in Peter Scarlet's voice sent a creep down the damp Dutchman's spine. "*Ja*, so. The German, Von Groot, shot a friend of yours and you started out with these five others to catch him."

"We got him," Scarlet gritted, "over in Makassar. We didn't kill Von Groot, but I wish we had. Bah. I was for law and order in those days, and we handed that German to the police. Do you think they gave him the rope? They did not. That Prussian racketeer was rich and he pulled more wires than a marionette show. He was worth a fortune and he bribed himself off. They gave him ten years in the colony prison up the Straits."

"Ach, I haff seen the prison. Myself, I would rather hang."

"Maybe Von Groot would've, too," the little curio-hunter snarled. "He did his ten year stretch and got out in 1923. But he was a dying man when he was turned loose. Caught the con sitting in a damp cell, I suppose. Anyhow he hung around Singapore for a couple of years under an assumed name, living like a prince on his dirty fortune. Then when he started coughing his head off he came back to this castle in the Moluccas. Finally he ended up in a hospital at Batavia. I was there when he died and the Dutch police asked me to identify him. No mistaking that ugly face. It was Von Groot, all right, and I tell you, I saw him buried. Three years ago that was. And I saw him buried."

Schneider, watching his friend's face, saw a queer expression in the curio-hunter's glare. The big Dutchman stirred uneasily. He didn't like the cabin door shut, and he didn't like the twilight beginning a purple shadow across the porthole. No more did he like the tone of Scarlet's whisper.

"When Von Groot died he left a fortune in gold behind him. Left it buried somewhere in his island castle. Listen, Wilhelm, who do you think he willed that fortune to?"

The Dutchman fretted. "I am an artist, not a mind reader."

"You may wish you're a mind reader before I'm done," the little American curio-hunter husked out. "Von Groot willed his gold to the six men who'd captured and shipped him to prison. Get it? He left that hidden treasure to McCord, Mallison, Giavetti, Captain Charlie, Dree and *me!*"

INCREDULITY FLARED in the Dutchman's moon of a face. "You say this Prussian murderer—this Von Groot—willed his money to the men who imprisoned him?"

"You can bet I laughed when his Chinese lawyers sent me a copy of the will," Scarlet rasped. "There it was, addressed to me in Von Groot's own handwriting. It said the money was in gold bars hidden in this castle down here. Five hundred thousand in solid metal. And the man of us who got to the castle first and found the money could have it."

"But, name of Godd—!"

"Wait!" Scarlet's voice dropped to the echo of steam. His fingers tightened on Wilhelm Schneider's arm. "I'm no fool. This will came by mail, reached me a month ago over in India. If you think I didn't smell a rattlesnake, you're wrong. Why would Von Groot leave us that gold? You bet. I beat it to the first telegraph office and tried to get in touch with McCord. The naturalist came first on the list of heirs, see? I didn't get in touch with him. His employers wired back to say McCord had gotten his copy of the will a year ago. He'd left for the Moluccas and nobody'd heard of him since."

Schneider grunted, "Maybe he got the gold and made tracks for America."

The little American curio-hunter shook his head. "Maybe. But how about Mallison. I shot a wire to the cinnabar outfit and found out Mallison had got a copy of the will a few weeks after McCord got his. Mallison had left to get the money, and nobody knew what had become of him. Not a word of him. Then Giavetti. The game hunter had been living at the Foreigner's Club in Penang. They didn't know what had become of Giavetti. All they knew was he'd started south for the Moluccas. That was a month after Mallison had started. Giavetti never came back, either."

"Bones of Orange!" Schneider panted. "Do you think they came down to this island, then?"

Peter Scarlet glared at the door, crossed the stateroom, put an ear to the panel. With a swift yank he jerked the knob. The door flew open with a gust of heat and a smell of nearing mud flats. But the deck outside was misted with dusk, and nobody was there.

The little curio-hunter closed the door with a mumbled curse; sat tense in his chair. "Swear I heard somebody breathing out there, just then." He dropped his voice another notch: "I'm not sure if those first three came down here, but I know Captain Charlie did. He left his schooner at Ternate and came on alone. His sailors told me that much. But he never went back to the schooner and his men didn't know where to look for him. But I know what happened to Dree. He got his copy of the will about six weeks before I got mine. And he *did* come down here. He brought a couple of British police with him, too."

"And he found the gold, this fifth man?"

Scarlet said in his teeth, "He did not. He left those Tommies down on the waterfront and went up to the castle by himself. They knew where he was going, and I suppose they thought he was safe. They waited all night, and when Dree didn't show up by morning they got winded and beat it to the castle after him. Only they didn't find him. Not a sign. Not a trace. They tell me they searched that place from bottom to top and there wasn't a sign of anybody. What's more that castle was empty as a tomb. Nothing but bats. The native islanders wouldn't go within a mile of it, either. And there it is. Five men dropped into nothing. Von Groot wills them a buried treasure and when they come to hunt it they go up in smoke."

It shook the voice in the little American curio-hunter's mouth, and it started a shudder in Wilhelm Schneider's scalp. But that wasn't all. Peter Scarlet, listening to his own words, felt the perspiration creeping on his forehead.

"The police had to give up. I talked with them up in Makassar just before I shot you that wire to meet me in Ternate. They didn't know a thing. All they knew was Dree had left to visit the castle and never come back. They agreed it was mighty queer about Von Groot's will. But there's something else queer with the will. Damned queer. A little message the dead man had left to steer us on. It said there was a portrait hanging on a wall in the castle. It said the one who wanted to find the treasure must first find the portrait. It said the man who had nerve enough to face this painting of Ludwig Von Groot, pictured with a gun in his hand, and look him squarely in the eyes—the man who had the courage to do that would find the gold—"

"What!" Schneider blurted. Sweat sprouted on his doughy face. His cheeks bulged at Scarlet and he rose like a balloon from his chair. "You say it is a portrait of Ludwig Von Groot hanging in this castle. A painting of him holding a gun in his hand?"

"That," whispered the curio-hunter, "was what it said in the will. I thought you'd be interested."

THE DUTCHMAN clutched at the table. "Bones of Von Tromp! Was this Ludwig Von Groot a tall man with a long bent nose, a head like a bald egg, a beard the color of a broom—"

"Then you remember him."

"But he told me his name was Vandeventer," the Dutchman panted. "Willip Vandeventer. He said he was from Flanders and had come out East for his health. In 1924, it was. He came to me in Singapore and wanted I should do a portrait of him, life size, with a pistol in his hand. A sharpshooter, he said he was, and the picture was for his mother in Antwerp. I painted him in three months, and he gave a thousand dollars and rushed away with the canvas. He was a murderer out of prison, and all the time he pointed that gun at me. Name of Godd!"

"It said in the will that the artist's name was Schneider and signed to the picture," Peter Scarlet growled. "I told you we were going to look at a masterpiece. The eyes, man! How did you paint those eyes?"

Darkness flowed through the porthole to drink up the last of the light. All save the shine of moisture on the Dutch artist's forehead and the gleam that was ambushed under the brim of the curio-hunter's helmet. The Dutchman was finding it difficult to breathe.

"I remember those eyes, Godd yes! I remember thinking they were terrible eyes, at the time. He coughed a lot, and every time he coughed those eyes would shine like candles of evil in some dark, heathen church. 'Paint them real,' he kept telling me, holding them wide open and staring. 'It is the eye that makes a portrait. Paint them real or I will not take the picture. Make them look alive.'"

Peter Scarlet swung to his feet; started for the door. "Schnei-der, we've got to find that picture of yours. Five men don't vanish for nothing. Von Groot didn't get that portrait painted for noth-ing, either. I don't know what you painted in the eyes of that masterpiece, but there's something damned strange about—"

Crash! The porthole smashed inward with an explosion of sharp fragments. Glass showered across the table. Something piccoloed *creeee* through the darkness, struck the door two inches from Scarlet's face with a thud. Quick as a panther, the little curio-hunter yanked the kris out of the wood, whirled, whipped out his automatic, sprang at the port.

But the lad who had crashed the glass to hurl that wavy Malay blade was quicker. Schneider, cursing and crowding at Scarlet's shoulder, saw the deck outside deserted to sooty gloom. Noth-ing but shadows, limp shrouds, and a thin malarial cat sitting atop a coiled hawser.

The schooner had stopped in a bay of dark glass that mirrored the ghost of a rind-thin moon. Forward the anchor chains were banging through hawse-pipes, and the schooner, swing-ing on the noiseless tide, came athwart a steep black headland. Somewhere a conch shell sounded a reedy horn note; bare feet pattered on the forward deck. Darkness steamed on the fore-shore under the mountain, but half way up the jungled eminence a clump of moonlit towers lifted silvered turrets out of the black.

"There it is," Scarlet snarled. "Let's go."

Crossing to the door, he kicked it open, stepped out on deck. Amidships the gangway was down; a bumboat piloted by a native oarsman rocked alongside. The French skipper with the peanut-brittle face stood at the gangway's head, innocent as a cathedral-window saint, lighting a cheroot.

The little American curio-hunter stepped forward to glare up at him.

"Listen, Frenchman, you don't speak English, but I've a feel-ing you savvy it. Maybe you'll savvy this. That's your pet cat on deck outside my cabin, and he wasn't scared of you to run away when you sneaked by to crack the glass and peg a knife through the porthole. Try that stuff again and I'll plant enough seeds in your belly to grow a cannon. And from now on keep your nose out of your passengers' business!"

Uppercutting hard, Peter Scarlet's fist struck the offensive nose like a boomerang. Frenchy, squalled, slammed over backward, bounced his head on a wheel-chuck and left it sleeping on its iron pillow, his face altered to strawberry fudge.

Going ashore in the bumboat, Scarlet cursed at his bruised knuckles. "Von Groot may be dead," was his somber promise to Schneider, "but I've a hunch it'll take more than a wallop to keep *him* down."

Dismally Schneider nodded.

CHAPTER II

SCHNEIDER TURNED THE story in his mind, clocking off the facts on pudgy fingers. No use talking, the more he thought of it the less he thought of it. The island was black as a hat except for those moon-washed towers half way up the mountain. Five men had come here and silently disappeared. Gold was at the bottom of it, and hate. More than one white man had vanished in a quicksand compound of gold and hate. But the gold was buried in this ancient castle, and the man who could hate was buried, too, dead for three years in his grave.

The little American curio-hunter read the puzzle in his Dutch friend's mind, and voiced his own thoughts. "I'd think Von Groot had come back if I hadn't seen him in his coffin with my own eyes. He made out his will just before he died, and three doctors in the Batavia hospital witnessed the testament. Then he instructed his Chink lawyers to mail the copies to the six of us one at a time and three months apart."

"It looks," Schneider whispered, "like he wanted to get you down here, each man after the other, *ja?* But what did he mean about the portrait and daring the man who found it to look it square in the eye? Why did he say the man who did that would find the gold? It gives me a chill to remember how I painted him with that pointing gun and how he said I should make the eyes alive."

Scarlet shook his head, frowning. "And the police who

searched the castle didn't find any portrait, either. I tell you, Schneider, there's something rotten in Denmark."

"Ja," the Dutchman panted, "and this is it, and I can smell it. I do not like this affair, my friend, because you are the last one in that will."

The little American curio-hunter didn't like it, either. A murderer dies and leaves his fortune to the men who sent him to prison. A Prussian gunman has his portrait painted and dares his inheritors to stare it in the face. Five men vanish to nothing in an empty castle where the picture is supposed to hang but doesn't. And Schneider couldn't help. The Dutchman had thought he was painting the canvas for a gallery in Antwerp; had not known his subject was a dying assassin just out of prison.

And the men who had disappeared down here weren't fools. McCord had been an aviator in France. Mallison, the cinnabar engineer, had fought and shot his way from one end of Asia to the other. Giavetti, the Italian hunter, was an expert with a rifle. Captain Charlie Loo had all the craft of a China Coast sailor, and Dree of the British consulate had been smart enough to bring his police. A dead man's will had lured them to this God-forgotten island. What fiendish web had caught them in the castle?

"There is something in that castle," Schneider whispered, "that puts a prickle in my palms. Look, Peter, there is evil in that place, as if it holds the island under a spell."

Queer how the moonlight silvered those old stone walls and the rest of the mountain steeped in black. The bumboat swam down a path of watery moonbeams, but the island was a cliff of pitch melting up into the sky and the castle seemed suspended in mid-air, its towers afloat in the night. In a spot like that anybody might disappear.

Scarlet touched the Dutchman's elbow and lowered his voice so the native oarsman wouldn't hear. "It's about a mile from the beach, by the looks. I'll go up alone, see? There's no reason why you—"

"Like hell you go alone. Don't forget I painted that picture—"

Scarlet could have grinned. Who said fat men weren't game? He reached to a pocket for his pipe, and encountered the metal haft of the kris. A cord of muscle stood out along the curio-hunter's jaw. He leaned up in the bumboat's stern and narrowed a glance at the schooner riding darkly at anchor in the roadstead behind them. That French skipper back there— why had he tossed that shiveree? Had he overheard the talk in the passenger cabin? Maybe a punch on the beak wasn't strong enough measure for that bucko quarterdeck bully. Might have been better to wing him.

"I'm getting soft," Scarlet berated under his breath. "I should've ventilated that rat with some lead."

But it wasn't the little curio-hunter's way, to shoot an unarmed man. Frenchy would stay put for a while, anyway. Gunfire would have brought the whole crew down on Scarlet's neck, at a time when he didn't fancy extra trouble. Better leave it as it was.

THE BUMBOAT was getting in. The mountain loomed to shut out the moon, and the darkness thickened with a smell of warm water, stagnant greens and mud. A lantern winked through the black to reveal a shabby dock where native sampans were tethered. Scarlet could make out the lime-washed walls of the go-downs, a rickety row of matchstick huts standing stork-legged along the beach. Drums boomed a muffled rataplan in one of the huts; there was the echo of chanting, a babbling rowdy song behind closed doors.

Scarlet paid off the bumboat man, and guided his sweating companion up the wharf. "A hell hole, for fair. The police that came down with Dree said there's a hotel up the beach, a joint where they spent the night. We'll stop in for a look."

Schneider lumbered heavily in the dark, his white coat flapping. "Me, I do not like this. It is too dark here. And our schooner out in the bay. How do you know the Frenchman is not mad at the little poke you gave him, and will sail off and strand us in this stench?"

"We'll hire the bumboat to take us off if he does. I don't think Frenchy'll haul out. I told him round trip, and haven't paid any passage money yet. The Frog ought to stand by."

He hoped so, anyway. Crunching up the cockle-shell path in the noisome dark, Scarlet knew he'd never made a port as foul. Pigs rooted in waterfront slime and mosquitoes hung in buzzing fogs. The headland cut off the breeze and the night was a steam bath. There wasn't enough light to see a match by. The hotel was a drunken frame building hanging on crooked legs over a stagnant inlet. Scarlet trailed the echo of singing to the dark veranda; thumped on the door.

Yellow light, gin fumes, tobacco and dope-smoke flowed from a crack that opened in the door, and a slant-eyed face appeared. Scarlet put his boot in the crack; shoved in. Here was the club house of the lost. Charter members squatted along the walls in doped indifference to the hopelessness of tomorrow. Brown men in rags, skin and bones. Skeletal women. Pipes and bottles, natives and mongrel dogs crouched together in decay. Not a few of the natives were blond in testimony of their one-time white lord and master. All were soaking drunk. The room reeked, and there were a score of little doors in back leading to further contamination.

The little American curio-hunter didn't waste time. "We're police," he announced to the Chinese doorman. "You the boss here?"

The Oriental's face was expressionless as a pie. Slant eyes empty as nothing. Hands thrust into the sleeves of a stained coolie coat, he bowed. "All same me, Hip Loy. Mista p'lice sit down. Maybe take nice room for tonight. Room, ladies, nice drink, all velly nice."

"Charming," Scarlet grunted, "but we've other business. You remember an Englishman named Dree who stopped here with two officers?"

"Young nice Englishman, nice fallow. White officers, nice

fallow. Englishman go away chop-chop. White officers stay night, go away chop-chop. No see."

There was only one table in a corner. Scarlet motioned the Dutchman to a chair; ordered whisky. This Chink wouldn't tell anything if he knew. The two Tommies had grilled him after Dree disappeared. Money might talk, though. He laid a handful of guilders on the table-edge.

"Listen, yella boy. Did a Chinaman named Captain Charlie Loo make port in here a few months ago?"

"No see."

"A man named Giavetti and another named Mallison?"

"No see."

Crash! The invisible fugitive was still fighting. "This way!" Scarlet bawled

"About a year ago, then. A white man named McCord?"

The pastry face appeared to be thinking. "Ah. McClord. Mebbe year ago. Stay here one night. Next day go away. No say where. No see. Nice fallow. Nice, tall fallow all same like in big hurry."

The money told that much, then. McCord had been here—nice tall fallow all same in big hurry. Scarlet passed a hand across his forehead and glared at Schneider. The Dutchman fanned his running face with his sun helmet. The room buzzed in a swimming smoke-haze, and a tightness came to the little curio-hunter's throat. He loosened the nerves with a long one out of the bottle.

"I'm going to visit that old castle up the mountain," he told the Chinaman calmly, "and I want some men. Guides to go along. What'll you take to go."

Expression came to the Chinese face then. Jaundiced pallor flowed up the jutting cheekbones. An oblique glare of fear sped from the pointed eyes. "Hip Loy never go see castle," was the squeaking response. "No see. All same native never go. No hire." He jerked his head to indicate his customers. "No can do."

Nothing faked about the fright in the Mongolian's pidgin chatter. Schneider, the Dutch artist, growled above his halted glass.

"What is wrong on this *verdammt* island? Why won't they go?"

"Von Gloot!" the Chinaman lisped low. "Him one time own island. Long time past go away to die. Him say nobody on island stop near castle or him ghost catchee killee quick-quick. No nice place, plenty bad. All same evil eye. Malay boy stop one time and see. Run plenty quick."

"What!" Scarlet was on his feet. "You say a Malay boy saw the evil eye in that castle? When? Where is he? This Malay!"

"Long two, mebbe three year ago. Malay see evil eye. Malay leave island go away quick. No see long time. *Aheee—*"

THE INN-KEEPER'S voice trailed off in a parrot-like

screech. Across the room a door had slapped open as if blown by a wind. Streaks of white flame squirted from the blackness beyond. *Wham!* Thunderstorm burst through that waterfront hotel. *Bam! Smash!* One of the singsong girls near the table gave a shriek, waltzed across the floor grabbing at smoke, fell and rolled. Lead whistled through blue mist. In Schneider's fingers the glass exploded with an astonishing smash, showering his face with whisky and throwing him out of his chair. Along the wall the huggermugger customers were piling and screaming, Scarlet's boot kicked the legs out from under the table, and he dropped behind the barricade with his automatic hammering. Flame-tongues lashed from the back room, the fusillade battering at the table-top, digging splinters. Hunched behind the wood, the little curio-hunter and the shouting Dutchman returned the fire, while the hotel owner hopped like a monkey to escape the crisscross barrage.

A blizzard of bullets swept the room, and the dead woman lay on her face and watched the ceiling with a gargoyle grin.

"In back!" Schneider squalled above the roar. "Get him, Peter! The back room!"

Leaning around the table, Scarlet drove a streak of shots at the flashing doorway. A close squeak when a ricocheting hornet tore the helmet from his head; then it was over as abruptly as its start. A muffled scream from the inner darkness of the back room. Sound of a gun clattering on the floor. Someone running and bumping in the gloom. The slam of an outer door.

"Quick!" Scarlet yelled at the Dutchman. "Outside!"

He was in the back room at a bound; through a rattan door that brought him standstill on a fan of beach. The gunman might have vanished in the starshine. Water lapping the sand made a quiet babbling; in the wall of jungle that lifted like a purple curtain at the end of the beach there was no betraying sound. Hunched in a wary crouch, the little curio-hunter emptied his pistol at the purple curtain, but there was only the rip of bullets tearing through vines, no answering cry. The fellow had made his fade-out.

Schneider circled the corner of the hotel like a trampling white elephant, puffing in fury. Nobody that way. Whoever it was had planned his exit.

"No use thrashing up the beach," Scarlet said in his teeth. "Might walk into another ambush. Come on."

Gun in fist, he led way into the back room. Light streaming from the front picked out the gunman's rifle where it had dropped, and revealed polkadots of blood on the floor.

"Nipped him, anyway," the curio-hunter growled. "If he hadn't been such a lousy shot he'd of riddled us."

Schneider dragged a cuff across a cut cheek, swearing hot Dutch oaths. "My face is full of powdered glass. *Ja,* I hope you hit that jackal where it hurt."

Scarlet snatched up the fallen pump-gun. "Winchester thirty-thirty. Somebody meant business. Let's see about the Chink."

The hotel had slumped to its original state of drugged lassitude. Outside the island night had resumed its steaming quiet, and inside, as if nothing had happened, the customers sat along the wall, watching the smoke with vacant, indifferent stares. In the middle of the floor the dead woman sprawled like a leather dummy, teeth bright in the lampshine; and the native denizens didn't care. She might have been there from the start of creation; might continue to lie there until she wafted away in dried shreds.

Only the Chinese hotel-man fussed. At sight of the returning white men, he skipped across the dead woman's legs to jig in front of Scarlet, his wax face jittering. "No arrest please. Hip Loy velly sorry. Catchee plenty hell, all time. That big niggah fallow all same plenty trouble, plenty bad."

Grabbing out, Scarlet caught the coolie coat by the scruff; shook the yellow man until his jaws rattled. "Big nigger, eh? You come clean on this, rat-face. You knew that gunman was in there, and you'd better come across before I knock the ivory out of your skull—"

"No likee," the celestial moaned. "No see niggah has gun. Big niggah him come here every night, take'm back room, smokee all time hashish pipe—"

"Where'd he go? Who is he?"

"Plenty bad devil, plenty black. Big black African come island long time. Island no likee. Black devil plenty tall with heap red hair. Live in jungle, kill plenty native. No good, all same madman—"

Scarlet cursed. Big Negro with red hair. A hashish-heckled madman somewhere out in the swelter of that night. It sent an itch down the little curio-hunter's necknape. He whirled at Schneider.

"Take the pump-gun. We'll get along. If we don't get started tonight we may not get started at all."

CHAPTER III

SCARLET HAD FOLLOWED some tough trails in his time, but nothing to match for evil that path through the jungly island dark. Faint starshine illumined the upward corridor through the morass, striping the muddy foottrail silver and black. Twisting like a tortured snake, the way wound up from the beach and lost itself in a forest of lianas and giant island trees. Pandanus, palm, sandalwood alive with creepers. Smell of orchids and bogs. Mats of hanging vine that reached down to brush a man's face like pythons uncoiling for a hold. Lizards sped in a willo-wisp shine underfoot, a malarial vapor poisoned the air, and the whole festering hothouse seemed to steam and simmer and brew a darkness thicker than mud at the bottom of the Tappkiang Well.

Once Scarlet halted to look back. Below the mountain the waterside huddle of huts had blotted out. The bay was a pond of ink caught in the armpit of the island, and the schooner was still there, small and ghostly as a mirage under the tropic moon. Scarlet remembered the kris in his pocket, shrugged, turned resolutely and pushed on.

"I don't like this." Schneider's face was gray. He made a gesture with the rifle. "Quiet like a cemetery. A madman is bad enough, *ja*, without the rest of it. And what did that Chinese son of hell mean about a Malay seeing the evil eye—"

The little curio-hunter shook his head, grimly. Might mean anything or nothing. Malays were superstitious as black cats. But some fool had wandered up to the castle and been frightened away, if the Chink's yarn was true. Von Groot had certainly put the taboo on the place as far as these cockroach-bitten islanders were concerned.

They plodded upward in tense-nerved wariness, guns alert where every moving shadow might prove an ambuscade. Scarlet, who had cut his sign across the worst littoral of Asia, could tune his ear to the dark and trace the slightest movement. For Schneider, fattened by the Bohemian ease of an artist's studio, the thing was hell. Sweat raced from every ounce of his two hundred and forty pounds, and he swore like an angry gnome. Five white men had vanished on this island. Already a razor-thrown knife had close-shaved Scarlet's cheek and a glass of Scotch had been shot from his own hand and a Negro maniac was hiding around the corner. But it wasn't that.

"What gets under my skin is Von Groot and the picture," he panted for the dozenth time, nervously sidestepping a log. "He told me his name was Vandeventer and he pointed a pistol at me and I painted like a fool. *Ja,* that scares me now I know who he was. A nice target I was with a brush in my hand smearing colors. And all the time his eyes how they were shining and he wanted them painted alive. Mynheer Godd!"

"It was in the will," Scarlet repeated harshly. "I could've dropped dead when I read how *your* name was signed to the portrait. I was wondering if you'd painted a sort of hidden map or something."

"I painted him pointing his gun and looking straight ahead. He would cough and his eyes would blaze. I colored them yellow and green. The eyes, they are the windows of the soul, my friend. Any artist, can tell you that. That is why we pull down the blinds on them and make them beautiful for our customers. But I painted the German's as they were and he was delighted. What could that mean in the will?"

"I want to know."

"But the police—the British who accompanied that fifth man here. They said they saw no picture?"

"They said," the curio-hunter husked, "the castle was empty."

IT LOOKED empty enough, all right. As if no human foot had tread there for a hundred years. Curio-hunter and Dutchman, coming up the trail, saw the walls grow taller against the stars, the towers, bartizans and turrets built by the red hands of buccaneers from Portugal, shaped frowning and massive in the Asian night. Vines crawled like green snakes across the masonry, moss and jungle flowers grew from cracks in the dark stone.

Narrow windows were like the blackened optic openings of a hollowed skull, and the moon poured its silver and silence down the walls. Far below lay the bay, and beyond that the horizon sweep of Molucca Passage. The castle made a stone giant crouching on the mountain, and the jungle huddled around in breathless fear.

"Shades of Wilhelm of Orange!" the Dutchman gulped. "That Von Groot must have been a tough one. To live in that bunch of dungeons even in daytime—"

Scarlet let a curse out of his beard. "I believe the Chink. No Molucca native would come within shouting distance of a place like this."

Only someone else was within shouting distance of that Portuguese *castillo*. Nerves twinging like the strings of a mandolin, the little curio-hunter pushed across a swampy ditch that had once been a moat, and led Schneider into the shadow of a granite archway. A rusty iron door stood ajar on broken hinges, giving view to a tomb-like hallway, a black crypt beyond. Stale wind exhaled from that inner midnight, dry, fetid as a belch from an underground catacomb. Schneider sopped wax beads from his forehead.

"*Himmel,* what a place? You haff got a light?"

The curio-hunter's pocket torch was tucked in his left hand. He thumbed the switch; shot a white ray past the dislocated iron door. It was as if that sudden ray of light had fired a bomb. *Wham!* Red flame spat a tongue in the black hall. That was the first Scarlet knew of another visitor. A bullet singing out of the castle, stabbing clean through his dented sun helmet. *Wham!* and a strip of cloth tearing loose from the Dutchman's sleeve. A third shot clipping through the trees.

At the first shot Scarlet had doused the flashlight; rolled aside, throwing Schneider out of the way. The little curio-hunter's automatic was pounding the second it left his belt, flaming a tattoo that lit the dark with sporadic lightning. Schneider sat in a capsicum bush, the pump-gun levelled on his plump knees, driving wild shots that banged like rivets on the iron door. The gunfire echoed up and down the castle walls, banged through corridors and inner rooms, played tag among turrets and roofs. A faint shriek sailed from the castle. The shooting stopped.

"Got him," Scarlet shouted. "He's running away."

Barefeet were scurrying in the dank hallway. Scarlet was through the arch like a miler, the flashlight streaking a path before his running boots. Wilhelm Schneider was not going to be left behind. The black hall rang with the sound of pounding heels. The pocket torch knifed a path through the stale midnight, reached out to discover a flight of stone steps leading into a narrow tower. Blood spots freckled the stairway.

"This way!" Scarlet bawled. "After him—"

Crash! The invisible fugitive was still fighting. The gunshot slammed from an upper landing—bullets zipped and bounced on the curved wall. Flattened to the steps, Scarlet and the Dutchman crawled up slowly, shooting their way. It was whale-hole black on that stairway, but moonlight streamed through windows at the top and showed a stone gallery hanging along the outside rim of the castle. Scarlet fired twice at a shadow fleeing along the gallery, and Schneider emptied the pump-gun. The shadow uttered a hyena's scream, twirled and fell.

They ran up jabbing ammunition into hot magazines.

The Negro was dead, doubled in a Z atop a cheap Henry rifle. He was big enough to fit the Chinaman's hysterical description. Scarlet didn't wait to question the color of his hair; the African's scalp, cheerlessly enough, was completely shot away. It wasn't a pretty sight on that high stone balcony under a horned moon with a smell of jungle decay in the air. Schneider's good-natured jowls were frogbelly color. Peter Scarlet wasn't exactly in an Easter mood. He turned the body over, gingerly, with a boot-toe.

"Looks like we've got the local idiot, right enough. Funny, though. I had an idea if the fellow attacked us again he'd lay for us back in the jungle. The Chink said no islander came up here."

"If you think I am sorry that beast is out of the way, you are crazy. Peter, I haff an idea. Do you think that monster Von Groot left this black behind with instructions to shoot your friends if—"

"I thought of that. But it doesn't fit. The Chink said this blackamoor came to the island two years ago. That's a year after Von Groot's death. And the fellow was rotten with a rifle, by the looks."

"He was too *verdammt* good to suit me!" Schneider fingered the rip in his sleeve.

"He might have sniped a couple of those men," the curio-hunter figured soberly, "but he wouldn't have nailed them all, That's what gets me down, I tell you. McCord, Captain Charlie, Giavetti, those others—crack shots the lot of them. Knew their way around. Not the sort to fall for any bushwhacking tricks." He clicked on the pocket light and sent a ray sweeping into the tower, a white circle moving along stone, ledges and slabbed walls. With the shooting died away it was quiet behind there. The stillness of vacant rooms, balconies deserted to weeds and dust. So quiet you could almost hear the whisper of wind in the cobwebs that hung everywhere like old men's beards.

"They came here hunting Von Groot's hidden gold, and they'd be on the lookout. I don't know where the treasure is and don't give a damn. I want to find those men. I've a hunch if we knew where that picture of Von Groot was we'd uncover something. We've got to hunt for it, Wilhelm. I'm going to find that painting if it's the last thing I live to do—"

Peter Scarlet didn't know it, just then, but that last sentence whispered fiercely through his beard, saved his life. Two hair-trigger deaths were waiting to catch him in that castle, and one of them was just around the corner. Hearing Scarlet's speech it bided its time. The other was somewhere inside, ten times as patient, a hundred times as crafty, more dangerous by a thousand. It had waited three years, and could wait forever. When the moment came it would never hesitate.

"We'll scour this German's rat-hole from top to bottom. That picture's got to be somewhere—"

Peter Scarlet gripped his automatic, stepped back into the tower, and walked toward that deadlier death.

CHAPTER IV

THE HALLWAY UNDER the tower was not a happy chamber. The blackness was that of a cave save where the flashlight's spot ran about the wall, ceiling and floor, searching doorways and stairs. Twelve-inch lizards, silent as thieves, dropped from stone sills and fled into crannies. Spiders large enough to catch and kill a bird dashed around on webs the size of draperies. Scarlet swore in a dozen dialects, and Schneider cursed like a Rotterdam whaler, breaking through those traps of evil silk.

There were four towers at each corner of the main room; a dozen corridors leading to darker caverns in the castle's base. In those stone compartments the adventurers of Lisbon had clanged their cutlasses in horseplay, smashed their wine jugs together at the name of Marco Polo, toasting tomorrow's bloodied seas and promise of loot. Headhunters had come there for samples and died to the crimson tune of blunderbuss and knife. In those underground crypts a Peking admiral, tired of white women, had set them to screaming with the torture of the thousand cuts. Then the cynical sailors of Spain, inviting the islanders to die for Madre de Dios and Toledo blades. Savage Dyaks squirming on racks operated by hooded Castilian monks six times as savage. Lastly the Prussian Von Groot with his modern murder methods and high-pressure racketeering.

The echoes of those long-past homicides seemed to linger in the turrets. Or was it wind? And footsteps in the lower hall traveled along the corridors in sepulchral mockery, as if a thousand men were walking.

Twice Scarlet halted to listen, sure he heard other boots. He cursed himself for nerves, turned, went on. They toured the main hall and found nothing. Breaking a trail through spider webs, they invaded a dozen smaller rooms; tramped across a crumbling balcony; climbed spiral stairways to tower-tops. Nothing. In the main hall, and down a flight of steps to a medieval dungeon where rusty chains lay like the bones of dead constrictors in shallow, stagnant pools. Otherwise the dungeon was empty.

The little curio-hunter's nerves were going on all six. Flashlight in one fist, automatic in the other, he poked into corners and pried at every shadow. The heat didn't help any. The Equator ran straight through that island jungle, straight through the castle. A Turkish bath in a graveyard. Both men dripped like wax. The Dutchman's clothes hung like the loose skin of a soaked and dreary pachyderm. He was an artist, a paintdauber, not a lover of haunted houses. He said as much to Scarlet, cursing uneasily at every turn, but he hung on doggedly, fisting the Winchester.

"Mynheer Godd! It is as if nobody was here since a million years. Do you hear that silence? That is Mother Asia brewing the spell of the East. That Von Groot must have owned the soul of a Nazi to like such a place."

If the other five had been there they had pulled in their tracks behind them. And it was no sport chasing a cold mystery trail through those sin-historied halls. Side by side, curio-hunter and Dutchman trudged up a tunnel-black stairway in the last tower. Flesh crept on Scarlet's spine. He didn't mind gun throwing and knife play—those games you could join in, and winner take all. But this hide-and-seek in a tropic manse, hunting men who had vanished and a portrait that wasn't there, playing a game with a man who had died without telling the rules—it got under Peter Scarlet's skin.

THE WHITE pocket ray went torching up the steps, picking out areas along the wall. Dust smoked underheel. Schneider wheezed, sweat, swore. Scarlet's jaw was clamped like a trap when they reached the top and discovered nothing but an empty lookout room, square as a box, with one barred window that looked across a court to the gallery where the dead Negro lay. He swung a damp hand, shaking cobwebs from his sleeve.

"We've covered the dump from the bottom up."

"There isn't any picture," the Dutchman pointed out dismally. "Where do we go from here?" His round blue eyes looked hopefully through the barred window toward a far-off patch of seawater. They couldn't get out of the castle any too soon to suit him. "Where now?"

For once in his life, the little curio-hunter had lost the move. He sent the flashlight whipping up and down the room. He didn't know what he'd expected to find in this tumulus of stone, but it hadn't been blank nothing. One man can vanish without a trace, yes. But not five. He tried to look back and envision what had happened to those five.

McCord was here first; had stopped off at the Chink's. Then Mallison, and a month later, Giavetti. Then Captain Charlie, and some weeks afterwards, Dree. They'd landed on the island; walked up the mountain to the castle. Had that Negro ambushed them, shot them down before they got here? If they came here where had—

Scarlet's mind stopped spinning with a snap. The flashlight paralyzed in his hand. Tension stiffened him like wire from toe to scalp, and a low cry bit through his teeth.

"Schneider, look at that!"

With that nervous agility astonishing in all fat men, the Dutchman spun from the tower window. "Wha—what!"

"That wall, there! By God, d'you see it?"

"*Ja*, I see it. A stone wall."

A panther couldn't have caught Scarlet going across that narrow room. "Like hell it's just a wall. See there? Look! There was a big spider web stretched across here from floor to ceiling.

And it's been broken to pieces. Something, lately, tore that web. Those cops who came looking for Dree never saw it. There's where the spider started to rebuild the thing."

An eight-legged, hairy monster scuttled to escape the torch ray. Landing like a mallet, the curio-hunter's gun-butt smashed the beast to an inky smear. *Thump!* The blow made a dull sound in the gloom of the turret. Scarlet whirled.

"That wall is hollow! There's an opening here, and somebody's been through. I thought the tower was a lot thicker than this room. Sound those stones with your rifle-butt! There's metal behind there! I'll try to locate the door—"

Panting oaths of amazement, the Dutchman pounded the wall. Scarlet slammed at the smooth-faced cubes. A sudden, mechanical rumbling filled the purple dark. A secret, grinding sound, as of an engine started by a touched spring. The tower shook. Clouds of gray dust cascaded from the ceiling. The wall was a flat shadow beginning to move, to groan, to fall away. Chains clanked, and the whole side of stone swung inward like the door of an ancient vault.

Schneider went backwards with a low cry of fear. Scarlet stood rooted in the black aperture, unable to close his mouth. A terrible and clammy wind gushed from the dimness beyond, and a cloud of bats blew squeaking and fanning from the door, filling the tower with a small storm of mousy wings. The little curio-hunter cursed and groaned. Schneider was a panting monument in chalk. Peter Scarlet wanted to move, but for the life of him he could only root there and stare. The scene in that room had turned all his muscles to ice.

CHAPTER V

"THE PICTURE!" WILHELM Schneider's voice was low as the seepage of gas. "The portrait of Ludwig Von Groot!"

Peter Scarlet had seen pictures before—terrible pictures: Kali, the Hindu goddess of Horrors, with her necklace of skulls and bloody jaws, painted on a temple-wall in Benares. The demon pictures in the palace of Ankhor Wat. The dreadful portraits in the Room of a Thousand And Three Sins at Negapata. Pictures painted by diseased, sin-twisted Asian minds.… But they were Sunday School Bible Studies, somehow, compared to that canvas on the wall of that hidden tower room.

The canvas hung in a metal frame that was bolted to the stone, the bottom touching the floor, so that it looked as if the man in the painting was standing there. So lifelike that the little curio-hunter had wanted to fling up his gun; and the artist who had wrought the likeness with brush and oils stared at his own handiwork in pop-ogled disbelief.

Shreds of moonlight sifted from a grating in the roof, slanted across the canvas and touched the painted features with a spectral shine. Ludwig Von Groot, long-dead, had come back to stand in that darkened corner and point his famous pistol across the room. The background faded into darkness; illumined with the wizard's lamp of the moon, the painted man stood out in ghostly relief. Von Groot in a faded khaki uniform. His great height broken by the stoop to his shoulders, his yellowish, bald head lowered, chin on chest, in a characteristic pose. The gauntly sinister face with its bent nose and scraggled, Teuton beard.

The eyes were the masterpiece. Schneider glared at the forgotten craft of his own brush and could hardly believe. Deviltry, mockery, a piercing, crafty gaze seemed to flicker from under those painted lids. For all the world as if those eyes were alive and aiming that painted gun. Peter Scarlet could have yelled. Only the cracks in the canvas, the tiny breaks in the dried pigments proved the thing's unreality. Moonbeams, shadows and artistry, the dark magic of that tropic island, seemed to make the eyelids flicker and the pupils glow.

Words from the dead man's will raced through Scarlet's mind. "The man who has courage to face the painting, look it squarely in the eye will find the gold—"

Slowly he moved across the threshold. A cry rushed from his lips. Pushing behind the curio-hunter's hunched shoulders, the Dutchman echoed that choky yell. There was something besides the painting in that moonlit chamber. Something that made Peter Scarlet's face stand out ashen in the lunar gloom. Where a patch of moonlight checkered the stone floor a hand was lying. A human hand, so dry, shrunken and leathery as to resemble a discarded pigskin glove. There was a wrist like a twisted stick and what seemed to be an arm, and a shadow beyond.

Icewater flowed down the curio-hunter's contorted face. His ears were aware of a faint, undertone droning sound, the ghoulish tune of myriad insect-wings. Worse than the flight of bats. The skin on that glove-like hand appeared to move, to hum and crawl. Scarlet clicked the flashlight, sick as he had never been in his life.

"Dree!"

In the ruthless betrayal of the electric spot, what had been the face of the English consular agent leered back with its cored, sightless eyes. The corpse sprawled on its back some ten feet distant from the picture, as if smitten there by a blow.

"Wh—why!" the curio-hunter's mouth worked to speak. "It looks—it looks like he was shot—"

The Dutchman grabbed Scarlet's arm, his fingers flabby. "Dear Mynheer Godd! Look! In that other corner. Another one!"

The flashlight wheeled in Scarlet's shaking hand. Another one, stretched out stiff against the wall, hands folded on his chest, a Martini rifle at his side. Insects rose in clouds from their unwholesome banquet, the tower room droned like a hive. Wilhelm Schneider cried out words that were not prayers.

"Mallison!" Scarlet moaned. "And—" the flashlight moved on its mourgish journey of identification, "Captain Charlie Loo. And my God! Giavetti!"

Laid in a silent row, toes pointed toward the grating and the moon. Carrion for the carnival of flies, their clothes in the mussy disarray peculiar to the dead, their limbs stiff, brown as mummies. The little curio-hunter could barely control his hand. It was quivering like palsy when it turned the flashlight on the last find—the little mound of rags and bones that had once been a man by the name of McCord.

Once before Scarlet had happened on such a scene. A chateau in war-torn France and a handful of Poilu sharpshooters, forgotten in the retreat of a last month's battle, marooned in an upper story and minced by shells. But here was no shrapnel-smashed chateau in France. Here was a tower on an island anchored in the heart of Asia, a castle abandoned in a jungle, a night as warmly silent as an opium dream. Here was a high tower room-in-the-wall, bare as a vault with a barred window in the roof, peopled by an oil painting and five silent dead. One by one they had come to the tryst; what diabolical fate had overtaken them there? The portrait of another dead man watched them with mockery blazing from its painted eyes.

"Von Groot!" Scarlet gritted. "He got them—somehow! Damn him! Damn that German hound of a—"

He started at the picture, passion knotting his forehead, his fist on the automatic white as a snowball. Schneider made a garroting sound in his throat, fumbling with the pump-gun. "Wait, Peter! I—"

"Attend, where you are!"

The words barked in the tower doorway. Dutchman and curio-hunter jumped around. Shadows surged in the gloom. The glint of hot eyes and bright teeth, wicked knives and the long shine of a shotgun. The shotgun pointed at Scarlet's head, and a voice like a file rasped commands.

"Stand so! One move out of you and you die!"

THE PEANUT-BRITTLE face out of Port Macquarie grinned like a skull. The French skipper's colossus shoulders filled the doorway, holding back a batch of tiger-faced Malay seamen. Bare feet that had brought them creeping up the tower without a sound, shuffled uneasily, anxious to jump and strike. The Frenchman moved across the threshold, snarling.

"A bas! Both of you. Drop ze guns! Up wiz ze hands!"

Wilhelm Schneider's rifle slid to the floor. The little curio-hunter let the automatic fall from his chilled hand.

"Frenchy!"

"Oui!" A vast grimace of mirth cracked the lumpy face. "Zis is me! Ze Frenchman who cannot speak or onerstan' ze Engleesh language. I heard you talking on ze schooner, messieurs. I catch ze story of zis castle an' ze gold that is buried here. Ho! A fortune, eh? I toss ze kris at you, hoping to scare you away. Ha, ha, you are too smart for Frenchy, eh? You punch heem in ze beak an' tell heem to savvy. I do not savvy—"

"You trailed us up here!"

The mariner bowed. "I am not ze man to laugh at five hundred zousand dollars in hidden gold. *Sapristi!* I have use for such treasure. While ze bumboat man is rowing you ashore, I call ze crew and we swim. Ho, ho! We swim faster zan you."

"I should have killed you," Scarlet said through his teeth.

"But ze worm it has turned," was the chuckle. "Already you

kill my negro serang, ze best mate I ever had. Observe, monsieur! I was waiting for you in ze Chinaman's little hotel. I paid monsieur—ze—Chinaman fifty guilders to tell you fake story about negro madman wiz red hair, in case I miss ze shots. *Oui,* my little cabbage, I miss zem in ze hotel, and zen I must run up here to ze castle an' wait. My negro mate, he miss you also." The Frenchman nodded at his bandaged wrist. "You hit me."

The little curio-hunter choked in fury. "Both of you lousy shots—"

"Perhaps, monsieur. But nevair do I miss at three feet! Keep up ze hands or I blow ze heads off both of you at once! I could have butchered you on zat outer balcony, too, my zigs. You did not know ze negro was leading you to ze place where I and zis little crew lay hidden." The big Frenchman talked slowly, tasting each word with vast enjoyment. *"Oui,* I had you zen, as now, in ze palm of ze hand. But I hear you say you must first find ze portrait to find ze gold. It is zen I decide to wait an' let you an zis Dutch elephant do ze searching. I see you have discover ze secret room for us, an' it only remains to find ze gold. *Merci, messieurs."*

Scarlet's arms were stiffening over his head, rage drying his cheeks. The Frenchman's sudden hold-up had cleared his mind from the shock of what he had found. The room stopped spinning; he could hear Schneider's frantic lungs; his hot glare leveled at the wolf-gang crowding the door. The skipper started a triumphant laugh.

"Go ahead and laugh," Scarlet advised him, husking the words in his beard, "but you'll laugh from the other side of your dirty mouth when you see what's up here in this room." Turning the flashlight in his upreached fingers, he sent a white ray streaking at the bodies against the wall, at the corpse in the middle of the floor. The things that had been hidden in black shadow jumped starkly into view.

The crew in the doorway staggered back. A yell burst from Frenchy's mouth. *"Sacre Nom du bon Dieu!"*

His glance switched, startled, at those frosty revelations—and

Peter Scarlet moved. Dropping his arm, he shot the full glare of the electric torch straight at the Frenchman's face. Dazed, the man fired. The shot tore at the ceiling. Scarlet and Schneider hit him at the same time. The Malays screamed and piled for the fight.

ARMS KNOTTED on the curio-hunter's neck. Cheek to cheek with the skipper, he fought to twist the man, the gun, three Malay faces and a thumb into a weaver's knot. Schneider was somewhere on the bottom, cursing in seven tongues. The tower trembled and rang. Dust boiled. In a maelstrom of legs, claws, knives, teeth, Scarlet, Dutchman, Frenchy and Malays swirled in that doorway where a stone wall had been. The pocket torch smashed to bits. Bats flittered in the roof. They fought to the top of the tower stairs, back to the doorway of the secret room, heaving, laboring, squalling like some travailing, many-legged octopus.

The painting of Ludwig Von Groot looked on. The mummified dead looked on. Midnight echoed to the conflict.

The fight carried into the secret chamber where the picture watched, and the dead men got into it. A weird and terrible embroglio of dead and living in the center of the floor, tangling and boiling in a patch of silver moonlight. Schneider was out of it, pinned flat by a dozen savage hands, kicking to free his feet from the ankles of something against the wall. Scarlet drove an elbow like a piston at the face from Port Macquarie, trying to throw the ox-like weight from his ribs and get a hand on the automatic he laid dropped. Frenchy put a hand across the curio-hunter's mouth; dug a thumb in his throat; pounded.

The little American's head rapped the floor. Skyrockets lit his brain. He struck twice at a grinning mouth—cracked his head on stone—went flat.

Malays piled over him; fastened him down. Schneider was spread-eagled. Cursing gorilla hatred, the French skipper soared to his feet.

"Hold zem! Tie zem up! Tie ze hands!"

Thongs lashed the little curio-hunter's wrists, knotting them behind his back. He could hear the Dutchman groaning, trying to fight; and he struggled in fury to throw his captors, but twenty arms held him in a vise.

The Frenchman swayed, towering in the moonlight. His face was black. Muscles corded on his jaws. He yanked a dagger from his belt, made a slice at the air. "Fight me, will you? Comedians!" He leaned at his captives. Foam bubbled on his lower lip. "I will blast off ze heads! I will cut ze windpipes! *Non,* but I have a better punishment—"

"Get out of this!" Scarlet snarled, "Get out of this, Frenchy, or I swear to God you're going to be sorry—"

"Sorry?" The big Frenchman screamed a laugh. He returned the blade to his hip and picked up his shotgun. "You are ze ones to be sorry, you and zis Dutch clown, *oui!* Put zem against ze wall," he swung at the sailors. "Line zem up zere with zere little dead friends."

Dragged across the floor, propped in a sitting posture against the wall, the little curio-hunter sat in helpless misery while the Frenchman kissed a bruised knuckle and laughed. The Malays huddled back in fear. At the other end of the room the portrait of a German killer watched the scene with ghostly amusement. Schneider glared rage.

"Swine! What are you going to—"

"I am going to teach a lesson, zat is what I am going to do. For both of you I am going to break ze legs!"

Scarlet's heart iced in his breast. "Break our—"

"Break zem with ze butt of my rifle," the Frenchman grinned, "so you will try to run on ze legs but ze legs won't run. Zen I leave you to sit up here in ze tower with your little dead friends to show you what you look like after while. Nobody hear ze yells you make, ze cries for water. Nobody come to ze castle. *Sacred Farceur!* but I teach you to punch ze nose!"

"You can't kill us, damn you! I'm the only one knows how to find the gold—"

"You forget I hear you talking on ze schooner, monsieur. First you shall watch me find ze treasure—maybe zat make you feel better after I go. I hear you say ze man who dares look in ze eye of ze picture finds ze place where it hides ze gold—"

For the life of him Scarlet couldn't move. Choking, sick, he took his eyes from the lust on the Frenchman's face; sped a helpless glance around the room. The Malays hung in the doorway like wolves. No help there. The picture—

Scarlet stiffened with a shock. He yanked his gaze from the painting and turned it on the big skipper's leer. Every hair on his scalp was aching, right then; the effort to speak low tore his throat.

"You win, Frenchy. But you haven't got the nerve to look it in the eye—"

The Frenchman whirled and was at the painting in a bound. Laughter blew from his teeth as he rushed at the canvas. His boots stamped the floor and he roared at the portrait face to face. "Me afraid of a—"

Wham! Something else roared. A thunderclap, ear-stunning smash. A roar that lifted Scarlet in the air—flung Schneider flat and yelling on his face. For the gun in the portrait's hand had fired! Flame lashed from the muzzle of that painted pistol, the gunsmash taking Frenchy full in the chest.

Spinning like a crimson dummy, the big French skipper came down the room. The Malays shrieked in the doorway to escape that whirling body; when it passed them by in moonlight they were gone. At the same instant hidden wheels had started to grind, and the sliding wall closed with a crash. Blown the length of the room, the Frenchman hit the far wall with a head-on slam. Loose bricks fell in a shower about his ears. He slumped to the floor, and a stream of bright yellow nuggets poured out of the wall and cascaded down on his broken neck.

The painting looked on with its mocking, level eyes. Smoke reeled from the painted gun. Dead and buried, Von Groot was still the marksman. But the eyes were blind. This time they had got the wrong man.

CHAPTER VI

PETER SCARLET CRAWLED across the floor to get the Frenchman's knife. Then it was only a matter of rapping the wall to open the door, and the little American curio-hunter and the beery Dutch artist from Islamahad got out of there. The tower was empty. The castle made no sound. Mountain and jungle slept. There were no Malays.

Wilhelm Schneider didn't wait, but Scarlet stayed long enough to cut the portrait from its frame, careful not to look it in the face. But the danger was over. There were rods and cogwheels like an iron skeleton behind the frame where the canvas had been, and the forty-five on the lever-arm was empty.

Sick to his heels, Scarlet fled the death-room. With the canvas clutched under his coat, he stumbled down the tower stairs. Schneider was waiting at the bottom, and together they raced for the door.

The moon had caught her horns in a pallorous green cloud, and the night was blackening as the two men plunged from the castle and down the mountain path. Just once the curio-hunter looked back. The mountain was blotted with midnight; the moon and the castle had gone.

"We'll send the police back for—for the others. The gold can go to their families, understand? I wouldn't touch it for a million dollars."

"The Frenchman found it all right, *ja!*"

"As Von Groot promised in the will," Scarlet whispered. "He'd hidden the stuff in that hole in the wall—set the picture across the room to look at it. The eyes stared straight at the spot where the nuggets were cached, direct line with the gaze. So if you followed that fiendish, painted stare—"

"But the gun in the picture, the painted gun," Schneider blurted. "Name of Godd, how—"

The little curio-hunter nodded. "I couldn't believe it, myself, until I saw it happen. But just at the last there, when Frenchy had us on the spot, it came to me. Those others—what had killed them off? Why had Von Groot been anxious for them to come to his dirty castle, lured them one at a time with a promise of treasure, told them to stand in front of his portrait? And then I remembered how Von Groot had been a gun-smith in Berlin. Frenchy was telling what he was going to do to us, and I took another glance at the portrait. Sure enough, the gun was painted, but the muzzle—the hole looked *real!*"

"You mean—"

"I mean the Devil took a back seat when he turned that Prussian gun-smith on the loose," Scarlet cursed. "He knew he was dying and he wanted to get even. He hated us. He couldn't kill us himself—then his portrait would kill us. Von Groot was an expert firearms mechanic. He planted a real gun behind the painting, a revolver loaded for six shots."

"Shades of De Ruyter!"

"Anyone standing in front of the picture and looking it in the eye would get it smack in the chest. McCord came first and caught it. Then Mallison, Giavetti, Captain Charlie Dree. Each one, finding the hidden room in turn, would see the others on the floor, wonder how in hell they'd been killed. Probably stop to examine the body and lug it against the wall. Next thing they'd do would be to jump at the picture, the way Frenchy did. And the curst thing would shoot them down. There was a lever under the stone block in the floor; the man's own boots would fire the gun. The discharge would start another mechanism and close that sliding wall. Von Groot—or his picture—would claim another revenge—"

Wilhelm Schneider cursed in his throat. They were breaking through the thicket that hedged the beach. The last of the moonlight made a wan pool on the sand. Out on the bay the schooner waited for a skipper and crew that wouldn't come; but the bumboat man was ready by the waterfront hotel. Schneider fastened a hand on the curio-hunter's arm. The rifle in his other hand was shaking.

"Give me that painting of mine—"

Scarlet handed it over. Suddenly the dark was shattered by the lambent crash of gunfire. The canvas smoked and blazed. Slippers came pounding up the beach, and Hip Loy the Chinaman was there.

"What are you doing?"

Scarlet gave the frightened Chink a grin.

"Killing a dead man," he said.

PORT OF MISSING HEADS

*The "Little Dog" laughed to see such sport—as one
by one those heads bobbed up in a far corner of India*

PROLOGUE

SOMETHING WAS MAKING Bradshaw uneasy. We were drinking out the evening on the naturalist's veranda—the fat man from New York, the tea planter and I—and I could see our host growing restive. Stirring at his swizzle. Hitching in his chair. Once he cocked an ear and listened to the tiger-striped dark of the compound, as if the dreaming Himalayan night had spoken out of sleep.

Below us Darjeeling's roofs were afloat in silver, and beyond the lifted jungle the moon-soaked peaks of the mountains made a Tibetan caravan in silhouette, motionlessly marching toward the moon. There was something Aladdin about the night. Such a night as only India could confect from a mixture of starshine and rhododendron.

The pinguid New Yorker was itching, too. "Got to get home. Leave for Calcutta tomorrow. Wall Street, you know. Office just cabled, and I've got to be there. Looks like stocks are going up."

The tea planter scoffed through his nose. "And once again we'll all lose our heads, I suppose, same as we did last time. People always go haywire when it comes to money, and they never learn. Give a fellow a sudden look at a million dollars and he always loses his head."

The New Yorker shook his chins, wise-eyed. "No, sir, I won't lose mine again. This time I'm going to profit by past experience."

The words had hardly spent from the broker's mouth when

an insulting, high-keyed outburst of laughter broke loose across the compound. A yapping, unnatural guffaw, exactly as if the jungle had overheard and was giving our friend the ha-ha, covering its mouth with a hand and half strangling in mirth. Our New Yorker stiffened with indignance. Knowing the source, the planter and I had to grin. But Bradshaw, the naturalist, did not grin.

In the lampshine the man's ordinarily cordovan face had misted gray. Leaping wordless from his chair, he darted into the bungalow, reappeared with a .30-.30 repeating rifle in his fists. On the veranda step he shot, felling a shadow that howled and rolled along the jungle's fringe. And in another moment he was back, stalking through the moonlight with a hairy, dead object dragged to heel.

"**WELL, BY** heaven," the New Yorker objected, "he's shot a dog."

"Not this time." Bradshaw dumped the beast aside, summoned the house boy to lug it away, stood there handkerchiefing his forehead. It was bigger than a dog, longer of leg. The head was wolfish with grinny fangs, and there was faint striping on the tawny hide, a short mane running the length of the arched back. A hyena, that was all. Scarce in that region but hardly dangerous, yet from the expression on the animal collector's face (and I'd seen him go after all manner of big game) you'd have thought he'd just bagged St. George's dragon. His hand, putting away the pump-gun, almost shook. Breath soughed out of him as he settled in his chair.

"Go on," he fended our concert stare of astonishment, "ask me. Well, I can tell you it's odd enough. Your conversation just now, and then that thing giving the laugh. Huh!" He looked as if a ghost had seen him.

We wanted to know why, and his color grayed the more.

"A laughing dog!" The phrase was a bone caught in the naturalist's throat, and he coughed it up with a grimace. "Then all this talk about people losing their heads over money. Getting a sudden look at a million dollars and losing their heads. It all ties up with this laughing dog business. I can tell you about some fellows out here who got a look at plenty more than a million dollars and lost their precious heads in every last sense of the word."

The pudgy New Yorker exhaled. "You mean really cut off?"

"Cleanest decapitations I ever saw," Bradshaw growled. "Madam-the-Guillotine couldn't have done any better. All except one chap who was a bit too short and got it just under the ears. They wanted a million dollars, those fellows, and that's what they got. There's a dog in the story, too, and a laugh. A last laugh that may not be the sort you'd like to hear." He pointed a brown finger. "It all happened beyond those mountains up there in a country called Bhutan. The first I knew of it was five human heads like a row of cabbages on your kitchen table. Stop me if you've heard this one."

Five human heads like a row of cabbages on a kitchen table! Bradshaw stared at the distant peaks as if the pretty tableau were visible there; and began.

CHAPTER I

THE MISSING HUNTER

AS FAR AS I was involved, it started with the disappearance of a man named Lewis Bellweather, and my being arrested for his murder; but there were four heads on the table already, and God knows how many before that, and the plot goes almost as far back as Adam snatching the first bite of apple from Eve. I've always had my own opinion about that apple affair. I don't think sex had a thing to do with it. I think Adam took the apple because he was greedy. So was Lewis Bellweather.

The man disappeared up there in those Bhutan mountains as completely as a dime down a grating. We'd left Gaugtok on the Indian border and were pushing over the Himalayas for Punaka, the capital of Bhutan, and we must have gone about a hundred miles as the crow flies and about six hundred miles by trail, uphill and jigsaw all the way over some of the tallest mountain I've ever scaled and the thickest jungle anywhere. Going upgrade all the time, you understand, like climbing a series of shelves. It took us twenty days to get where we were, considering the rains and the fact we had to chop a path most of the way, and Punaka was another week distant.

Then Bellweather walked from his tent one night and vanished. Presto! Horse and all. A needle in ten haystacks would have been nothing by comparison. I beat all over the bush with the gun boys and we didn't find a trace. Alone he couldn't have gotten far in that jungle-wedged wilderness, but there wasn't any lost and found department in Bhutan.

He was gone like Robin Hood in the green. Off the map where there wasn't any map.

I remember the day was Friday because Bellweather didn't eat meat; and I remember not feeling very sorry, because the fellow had been pretty unpleasant. Always accusing the natives of being superstitious, ragging them for their customs, driving them like a muleteer and bellowing at them to hurry. He was a tall, thin man with a gray, tight-lipped face and secretive eyes behind suspicious pince-nez glasses; made me think of a bad-tempered algebra professor. Splenetic and precise. Everything had to be just so, we must go this way and that way, stop for lunch under such and such a tree, climb such and such a cliff, and I, who was supposed to be a sort of guide, just tagged along.

It was supposed to be a hunting expedition; Bellweather staked the money, hiring me for dragoman. After white rhino, he said, to donate to the Museum of Natural History. We spotted plenty of game, but when we didn't flush any rhino his impatience mounted; nights he sulked alone in his tent poring over books. He wasn't what you'd call sociable, and I confess I didn't mourn the lost companionship when he walked out that Friday night. But of course I was worried as the devil.

THE DISAPPEARANCE of a man up there in Bhutan, especially a white man, wasn't anything amazing. Look at your Atlas. The country hangs up there like a vulture's nest between India, Nepal and Tibet. As a wilderness it's got everything. Jungles and snow-capped peaks. Valleys hot as the tropics under peaks of blue ice. Look at your encyclopedia. "The exact extent of the territory remains unknown. Population semi-Mongol mixed with blood of Hindustan. Largely uncivilized. Religion an offshoot of Llamaism, pagan."

Likely enough spot for a white man to disappear; it was Bellweather's reappearance that got under my skin and gave me the jitters. I stood by two weeks thinking the man might blunder back to camp but certain he was dead of sunstroke, tiger-teeth or tribesman's bullet by that time. On the morning I was packing to leave, a little squadron of British-Indian police blew hell bent for leather into camp. Night and day they'd ridden; their horses were badly lathered, and the men came at me with yells.

First to dismount was a chunkish Captain Jones, followed by an escort of native troopers led by a Sikh lieutenant, red henna whiskers cut Hughes-pattern, big Moslem turban, named, of course, Abdurahman. Abdurahman covered me with an automatic while Jones opened proceedings by hauling a gaudy document all stamped over with British lions from his tunic,

The major's gun
clicked like a
sewing machine

muttering something about extradition and tapering off with, "You're wanted for murder."

"Just who did I murder, if you don't mind?"

"Sorry, old man. American citizen supposed to have accompanied you into Bhutan—one Lewis Cornelius Bellweather—"

"Supposed to have accompanied me?" I hollered. "He did accompany me—" Then I realized Mr. Bellweather wasn't there to back me up, and the short hairs began to bristle on my neck. I assembled my bearers with a yell. The whole batch of them had been acting queer since Bellweather's excursion into space; in fact they'd acted queer from the minute we'd entered Bhutan. But they stood by me well enough, testifying to Bellweather's so-called accompaniment with high-signs and groans.

Jones glared. "You say he disappeared two weeks ago Friday from this here camp? Well, the police found him, or what's left of him, twelve days ago Sunday in Gaugtok. You'd better come along."

It was funny, but not amusing. I wasn't a bit sorry to be leav-

*The strange duel
lasted fully a minute*

ing Bhutan, but it was an oddish departure, believe you me. We started for Gaugtok, leaving Abdurahman of the red beard behind with a couple of troopers to X-mark the spot, hunt around for any possible clues and then, after a week or so, come home. Jones said, "anything I said might be used against me," and we rode out of the mountains like clamshells. I had plenty of time to do some thinking, and maybe you can see what I saw. Bellweather vanishes Friday in the heart of Bhutan. The following Sunday the police find "what was left of him," as Jones so picturesquely reported it, in Gaugtok. How in Tophet had Bellweather's remains returned to Gaugtok in three days?

IT WAS clear as mud, and the roil hadn't settled when we crossed the frontier into India, days later, and I ended up in a police station facing the Deputy Commissioner. Meet Major Colin Smythe. You know the sort if you're acquainted with the colonies; his prototype sits under a punkah-fan, thumbing official dossiers and drinking whisky pegs at desks all over India. Typical British administrator, spruce as salt and pepper, blunt jaw shaved to the blue, tired around the eyes, but all for tea and the King. Duty. Efficiency. What's sporting. England-will-muddle-through. A life built of military uniforms, mess jackets, hard work, hard pay, climbing the ladder of petty civil service jobs to a minor executive position, ending in retirement with a curry-and-rice liver and a house in Cotswold. Character!

That was the word that always struck me on meeting Smythe—character. And there'd been times when, not having too much character myself, it had annoyed me a bit. Rule a bunch of frontier natives long enough and you get a little too Napoleon-like for me. A fellow should go on a bender once in a while.

And then I could imagine Smythe turning purple and bawling the daylights out of his batman on a matter of boot-polish.

Well, he was chief executive officer of that God-lost frontier district, and when I found him waiting for me in Gaugtok he looked more stern than purple, and I knew the matter was damned serious. He kept me waiting in a fidget while he inspected my pack train and made a Swiss watch inspection of Bellweather's luggage. Finally he was back at his desk with police note-books and pencils everywhere and his toughest Deputy Commissioner expression on his face. He questioned me closely on every point of the hunting expedition, and I was stewing hotter by the minute with apprehension and bewilderment.

"You insist you were five days from Punaka, deep in the Bhutan mountains, when Bellweather vanished?"

"For the twentieth time, and my bearers will insist the same."

He tapped an impatient monocle on his Covenanter's chin. "Yet we find him three days later here in Gaugtok. Impossible, what?"

"You mean," I snarled, "you think I must have killed him hereabouts before we set out. Well, Bellweather trailed with me for twenty days going in. Unless, of course, there are two Lewis Bellweathers. One of 'em vanished from that mountain camp, see? How could his body—"

"I didn't say anything about a body," Smythe snapped, squaring up out of his chair. "Please come this way."

He led me past a Sikh policeman into a little back room where a few bars of light were sneaking through dingy screens and a slow fan was whispering under the ceiling. Nothing in it but ourselves, a shabby pine table and some lumpy objects under a white tablecloth. A *chipkilli* lizard fell from the ceiling as we entered, shattered its brittle tail and sped down a crack like a scared thought. Giving no word of abracadabra to open the act, the Deputy Commissioner stalked to the table with a faint chinking of spurs, yanked off the white cloth with a flourish, like a yogi magician disclosing some neat legerdemain.

PERHAPS HE expected me to bellow a confession on the spot, and believe me if I'd had any crimes on my conscience in front of that Third Degree I'd have bellowed them. Whew! To this day I can see those five heads in my dreams. Lined in a row and ticketed like prizes at an agricultural exhibit. Number One was plump and bald; Number Two had a white handlebar mustache; Number Three was hook nosed; and Number Four had got it just under the ears. All were brown, expressionless as coconuts, but Number Five, nicely severed at the neck, took the blue ribbon as far as I was concerned. Although the features were not in absolute repair, the gold clasp of the pince-nez spectacles remained clamped between the secretive eyes, and the ill humored mouth was recognizably open on a silent curse. You get to know a face after twenty days with it in a wilderness. No mistake about this one. Unquestionably it was the head of Lewis Bellweather.

I fancy I was greener than lettuce. Some of the God-save-the-King had leaked out of Smythe's doublet, and he looked a trifle green himself. Only for a second. Then his eyes on me were hard, shiny gray disks, calculating as Sherlock Holmes; he was Deputy Commissioner again, stiff as Cromwell. Jerking a riding crop from his boot, he arranged his shoulders and assumed the dry composure of a lecturer in anatomy class.

"Number One," pointing the stick like a wand, "Number One—Jan Stroon, Dutch silk buyer, reported missing from Batavia, Nineteen Twenty-Nine. This head discovered in Gaugtok, Nineteen Thirty."

The wand tapped the head with the white mustachios. "Number Two—Sir Enoch Temple, K.C.G., Fellow of the Royal Geographical Society, reported lost during expedition in Persia, Nineteen Thirty. Head discovered in Gaugtok the following year."

The wand dragged my wincing gaze to Number Three. "Israel Grusbaum," the Deputy Commissioner introduced crisply. "Levantine gem merchant. Seems to have done business in Bombay, year of Thirty-One. Last seen alive, Saigon, Indo-China. Head discovered here in Gaugtok two years ago."

It became apparent that the town of Gaugtok, away up there on the India-Bhutan border, was the port of missing heads. People vanished a thousand leagues away and their heads turned up in Gaugtok police station. No wonder they called the building headquarters. All right, the wand tapped that Number Four specimen that was halved just under its ears. "Marcus Lunt," my informant hurried. "German air pilot reported lost last year in Berlin to Tokyo race. Plane last seen over Afghanistan, flying east. Head, identified by old cranial fracture, found ten months ago in Gaugtok. Now then," the British police officer drilled me with an eye-to-eye glare, "I must ask you, sir, if you can identify Head Number Five."

I whispered, "That's Bellweather, for a fact, but *I* didn't chop it off, and I never saw those others before or want to see them again." It was one of those occasions when you had to jest or collapse. I said angrily, "Who do you think I am, Henry the Eighth?"

The Deputy Commissioner's voice was brittle, scissoring through dried lips. He answered me with a question that tugged at the roots of my hair. "Look here, Bradshaw. Did you ever hear of the Little Dog?"

CHAPTER II

A WEIRD LEGEND

NOW YOU COULDN'T be long out in Asia without hearing of the Little Dog; sooner or later the story got you by the ear. It was one of those indigenous grandfather-to-son legends that persist through the East like the gold chains of Menelik yarn in Abyssinia or the Seven Cities of Cibola in the Caribbees. This legend was older than Noah's Ark, and sung in all the hugger-mugger dialects of the Orient, originally Dravidian, I fancy, touched up by later Buddhistic embellishments.

At any rate, through all manner of versions, the main theme was the same—one morning during the dawn of the world, Buddha (Allah, or Brahmah, according to your faith) took his dog for a walk over the mountain. Just what mountain was selected for this post-prandial saunter was one of the fine points that kept the later theologians chinwagging. It wasn't any ordinary mountain, and it wasn't any ordinary dog.

According to legend it was a Little Dog, and true to Asian rhetoric which says one thing and means precisely the opposite, this Little Dog measured fifty times the size of your average hound, about ten feet tall, with eyes like blow-torches and a mouth bigger than a cave. A god wouldn't be owning any mongrel. The Little Dog of Buddha's was no pooch, not by a jugful. Besides being of gigantic proportions, it was made of solid gold. And those were shabby details when it came to the Little Dog's tongue, which was nothing less than a diamond—a whopping big uncut diamond as chunky as your foot, bright as fire, so that when the Little Dog opened his mouth the blaze was as from a million glowing suns.

What was more, this celestial Great Dane's mouth was open just about all the time, for he was a good Little Dog with a dandy sense of humor and spent his time laughing and laughing. Who wouldn't with a bonanza like that for a tongue? That was the dog which came striding over the mountain with its saintly master, and naturally it stopped beside a giant tree.

Buddha was always coming to rest under a *bo* tree; and while they were shading themselves under this great monarch of the forest, the Little Dog fell asleep.

Buddha tiptoed off somewhere on errands of his own; Night unpinned her dark, starry cloak across the hills and hung a great yellow lantern in the sky.

Enter the human element. Bandits. Mortal men, of course, with their eyes on the main chance. There was Fido asleep with his mouth open and that fifty-million-karat diamond tongue lolling and twinkling in the moonlight. Do you think those men gave a toot because it was Buddha's pet? Not they! These dawn-age hoodlums yelled with desire when they saw that brilliant. They attacked Buddha's pet with rocks and arrows, while the leader of the mob rushed forward with drawn scimitar to hack off that precious tongue.

That was just too bad for the leader. The Little Dog woke up. A whole slew of arrows were sticking in his back, but you can't kill a solid gold dog with arrows, even in an Oriental fairy tale. And in his haste to get to the diamond tongue, the leader tripped over his own feet and fell ears over teacup.

The sight of that bandit taking a flop struck the Little Dog right on the funnybone. The Little Dog roared with laughter and bounded at the gang leader and bit his head off with one snap. Then he snapped the heads off the rest of those robbers, one, two, three, and when Buddha re-entered the scene their bodies were piled up like cordwood. My, how the Little Dog laughed!

But alas for the genial Little Dog; one of the gangsters' rocks had broken off his left hind leg, and he couldn't get away from under the giant tree. He was too heavy even for the immortal Gautama to lift, which put Buddha in such a fury that he turned in rage on lustful mankind and set up an unalterable decree. Henceforward human avarice should always be repaid with misery, and every time the Little Dog laughed, or any dog anywhere laughed, the grasping mortal within earshot would lose his head. Let greedy Man beware of the Little Dog, lest his feet trip over his greed and the Little Dog would laugh and he would die decapitated!

THAT WAS the legend of the Little Dog, and it's not a bad parable in its way. You can see how every thieving native would shake in his sandals at the sound of a hyena under the moon. But here's the point. The story claimed that somewhere on some forgotten Asian mountain the Little Dog still sat under his *bo* tree, mouth open and laughing with that tremendous diamond tongue ashine in the sun. Then about ten years ago some archaeologist authenticated reports that such an image had been built back in the days of the Bharatas, present location unknown, and that was enough to set every crackpotted fortune hunter and renegade between Aden and Port Arthur looking for the thing. The prize, of course, being the diamond tongue; and to hell with Asian superstition.

I'd never taken that dog story seriously, myself. If there'd ever been such a diamond-tongued image, its pedigree was certainly exaggerated, while the idol itself had probably been carted off long ago by Genghis Khan or somebody and broken up into job lots. Yet the legend persisted around the Indian littoral, the natives took the parable as gospel truth, and the idea gave me something to chew on in that frontier police station where those five human heads looked back at me from the table. Smythe wasn't going to tell me those men had been decapitated by a myth?

"Not exactly!" he gritted at me.

I asked him if he believed there was such an image around.

"Now," he watched my face, "we're getting to cases. It is known that the Dutchman, Stroon, once tried to finance an expedition to hunt the Little Dog. We also know Sir Enoch Temple made researches on the subject. Grusbaum and Lunt, is it too impossible they were after the thing? Is it too impossible," he caught my arm in a sudden twist, "that you and Bellweather were hunting that confounded thing?"

Bradshaw

Flesh crawled on my necknape. "Bellweather said he was after rhino," I cried.

"Then take a look at this; I found it in Bellweather's duffle," Smythe clipped out, snatching a book from his tunic and thrusting it at me, cover opened to the flyleaf. I saw it was a novel by Kipling, one of those books Bellweather had sulked over in his tent. And I saw something else. You know how a man will scribble on a pad while telephoning? Jot down the subconscious from his mind? I don't suppose Bellweather had realized what he'd scrawled, but his drawings in the light of that abominable inquest were plain as day. Dogs. Crude artistry, yet unmistakable. Roughly sketched by a pencil moved in thought. Little dogs sitting at all angles under trees, each dog minus a hind leg.

My eyes jumped back to Bellweather's fresh-picked head, but a mind reader couldn't have quizzed it by this time. I stared at Deputy Commissioner, Major Colin Smythe. "Great Lord! He *did* act almighty queer on the trail. As if he had something up his sleeve—"

Smythe nodded grimly. "I believe your story," he told me in sudden decision. "I've got to take you into my confidence, Bradshaw. There's a beastly uproar about this whole affair. Home governments of these slain men have been raising the devil, and we're straining every nerve to solve the cases. Consider the thing. Five heads popping up out of nowhere in this village. No bodies found. Gad! We blamed the Thugs at first, but *Thugee* has been wiped out in this district since Lord Roberts."

PERSPIRATION STOOD on his temples. "And why are the heads sent to Gaugtok? Four of those men weren't within miles of here to begin with. Stroon last seen in Java. Sir Enoch in Persia. Bellweather's the sole one ever seen here alive. Naturally I had to warrant your arrest, y'see, as the first living witness I've had to work with. We've grilled the local natives to perdition. No clues there. They insist the Little Dog brought those heads to town as a curse. Local superstition the Little Dog once walked through this village with Buddha.

"Nonsense, eh? Yet we find three of the victims had some sort of interest in the bloody legend."

The man's eyes kindled in mounting anger. "But the hill tribes of Bhutan believe in the thing. Every blighter in Bhutan is a potential headsman. I think these white men sneaked into their territory hoping to find that beastly image. The Bhutanese caught 'em and sent their heads over the border as a warning. British prestige is at stake, sir! Our natives go off the handle on this sort of thing. Frankly, the Bellweather head is dynamite, and it's a mighty delicate situation for the police. How'd that—that head get here from the Bhutan hinterland in three days? I tell you, Bradshaw, I'd thought your story might solve the thing. Now there's only one answer left."

I could see it was an answer the Deputy Commissioner didn't want, but I couldn't think of any substitutes in that mourgish atmosphere.

"Airplane!" he burst out savagely. "It's the only solution. Bell-weather's head must have been smuggled across the border by plane!"

I gasped, "An airplane? Up there in Bhutan?"

"And," the Deputy Commissioner slashed at a fly with his stick, "there's only one in the whole country. Owned by the Rajah in Punaka. British government sold him a ship way back during the War. That Rajah's a mysterious devil and he hates the British *Raj* like poison. He beheaded those men and sent their heads here by air; how else could Bellweather's reach here in three days?" Smythe's voice broke on an oath. "I want your help," he demanded abruptly. "Make it worth your while, too. There's a thousand pounds reward posted on this case."

I asked dismally, "Where was it found?" nodding at what was left of Bellweather, half expecting an air mail stamp and the local post office. Smythe's jaws tightened on another wrench.

"Right here in town," was his wrathful answer. "Same spot all of 'em were found. Little river flows from the rocks at the edge of the village and passes behind this station house. You know it? That's where these heads were discovered. Chucked into the creek behind our police house!"

He steered me to a back screen for a look. I looked, and then both of us were looking. Maybe you think we weren't! The stream slid coffee-colored between sluggish flats of cracked mud not a dozen yards behind the police bungalow, and where it shallowed and widened a bevy of stork-legged natives in diapers were wading in the lavender twilight like excited birds. A taffy-colored zebu, dazed in the evening heat, looked on with stupid eyes. Not so stupid as our eyes, right then. The waders pointed and screeched. Natives dashed out of their cowpad huts, yelling. Smythe flung open the screen and a torrent of howls came into the room. Jones and two troopers came running from the front of the building. The racket mounted in the dung-smoked India dusk.

"Great God," Smythe gasped, "look at that!"

Braver than his brothers, a native had fished something out of the shallows; was holding it arm's length aloft. The brown crowd shrieked. "Wah!" Slanting sunset light took the object in the face. It had been in the water some hours, and mud and silt poured from the red henna beard. It was the head of Abdurahman, the Sikh lieutenant we'd left back there in Bhutan. I stared at those mountains towering behind the village, silent, brooding crags, and the sweat bubbled out on my face.

We were off for those gooseflesh Bhutan hills—Major Smythe, Captain Jones and I—before the moon was up.

CHAPTER III

AN ENGLISHMAN'S COURAGE

YOU'VE SEEN CALCUTTA and electric cars and race tracks
out here, and maybe you think the tourist catalogs cheated
you—India looks too civilized. Remember, there's British India
and Native India—about six hundred rajahs and nawabs ruling
territories on their own, tied to King George by the merest
thread. Your rajah may sport a twelve-cylinder racing car, but
he still hunts tigers by elephant and what he does in his palace
is his own sweet business and liable not to be so sweet. For this
prince of Bhutan to own an airplane wasn't as unlikely as it
sounds, despite the fact that of all the states tied to the Indian
Empire, Bhutan's thread was thinnest, the country most savage
and least known.

I hadn't gone a mile that night before I regretted it. The country had been wilderness before, now it was Beyond of Beyond.
Our three-man expedition was swallowed in those hills like a
three-mouse expedition swimming seaward into green waves.
Jungle closed behind us in silent doors, and the memory of that
police house exhibit began to work along my spine.

Smythe made no bones of the fact we were walking hobnailed
on eggs. His Britannic Majesty had scarcely a breath of authority
in this Himalayan feudal domain. Diplomatic reasons forbade us
an escort of soldiery, and almost anything was bound to happen.
But Smythe was mad. His jaw was a cobblestone. Abdurahman's
ghastly homecoming had been the last straw, the last smirch,
you might say, cast at British law and order; as if the killers had

spat defiance at Smythe's creed; and the Deputy Commissioner, outraged, swore to find and punish the guilty if he had to crack the Forbidden City single handed without a warrant.

Jones, too, was raging to go. I thought of two Angels of Vengeance riding to batter in the doors of hell, and I cursed myself for going with them. Smythe begged my assistance, saying I knew the dialect and the trail; but policing Great Britain's borderline at a chance of losing my noggin was no business of mine, and my hair telegraphed warnings to stay home.

I don't know why I went. Yes, I do. It wasn't the reward, either. Away down inside of me somewhere, I suppose, there'd started a gnawing curiosity about that Little Dog angle to the case. That was it, and I may as well admit I wanted a look at that thing. For a thousand years the story of the fabulous canine had stirred the imagination of the East; all the globe trotters to foot-track the Asian back-trails had whispered of the beast. I was increasingly certain Bellweather had engineered something more than a rhino hunt, somewhere in Bhutan he'd scented the Little Dog. I began to speculate.

Awake, I had enough sense to remember the heads on that kitchen table, but nights I dreamed of a golden dog with a tremendous diamond tongue, and my dreams caught fire from that diamond. A week of trail pushing with those two lock jawed British policemen, breaking the silent jungle wall in silence, thrashing a dark path up the mountains, had my nerves honed to fine edge. Every time I thought of what had happened to Bellweather and the rest, the picture of the Little Dog hung itself in front of my eyes like a mirage.

I began to be sure Bellweather had been after the gem, hiding his purpose behind a hunting license. Finally I was as certain of it as Major Smythe was certain the Rajah of Bhutan had caught Bellweather, sent him to the chopping block and, as in Abdurahman's case, shipped the souvenir to Gaugtok by plane.

"Flew 'em to India by night," the Deputy Commissioner had it figured. "Landed near the village under cover of darkness and left 'em behind in that stream. I'll show the monsters what it means to play that sort of game with the police!"

"The rotters," Captain Jones would snarl. "Bloody fiends!"

A NICE little trip to be taking, wasn't it? I want to say those Englishmen had courage, starting through those mountains as they did. Then we met the two troopers Jones had detailed to stay with Abdurahman. They were racing for Gaugtok with the news of the Sikh's disappearance, and their story, boiled out of them by Smythe's rigid grilling, didn't help matters a bit. It seemed the unlucky Abdurahman had walked out of camp just as Lewis Bellweather had walked out on me, pulling in his tracks behind him, going at night, leaving no trace. The two *sepoys* didn't know what had happened to the Sikh officer and they burbled in terror when Smythe told them, quitting their jobs on the spot and spurring for home.

I guess the three of us had the blue jitters when we reached the camp which marked the jumping-off place of those last two disembodied men. Storming rain when we reached the spot, the jungle a quagmire hopelessly blotted, all of Scotland Yard couldn't have uncovered elephant prints. Nothing for us to do but turn in, sloshing into dreary pup tents for a miserable night of it. Early next morning the cloudburst was gone, so Jones decided to go, too. It was sun-up when Smythe came fisting into my tent, his face turned to bone, eyes lit with ferocity, to tell me the police captain was nowhere to be seen.

"Walked out of his tent last night. Walked, I tell you. His footprints go into the bush, and he can't have gone far, and if he did it means somebody took him. We'll pull this jungle down piece by piece, Bradshaw! We'll comb the mountain on a ten mile radius. We'll hunt till the end of the week, and if we can't find Jones by that time we're going to Punaka!"

The end of the week, Smythe and I set out for Punaka.

I WON'T try to tell you about that trail to Punaka because I can't remember the road, and I'm not even sure the place we reached was Punaka. I was too scared to do any map-mak-

ing that trip. You know I
was! The country we climbed
into was hell. Jungles of
thorn where every bush put
out hooks to claw us back.
Regions of boulder and rock,
huge misshapen stones that
littered the landscape like
petrified hunchbacks in a
necropolis of the dead. Black
cañons and forbidding crags,
forests ghostly in stillness,
great time-old cliffs that
stood like sombre skyscrap-

Major Smythe

ers in the high, thinned air. Those mountains cast a shadow. The
country didn't want us there. It blistered us by day and froze us
at night, slashed at and threw us back, closed walls of jungle and
granite around us, lost us in its uncharted maze.

Smythe pushed on. His Saxon jaw was a battleship and his
eyes were like steel guns. He hung his Webley across his lap and
set his spurs, wrapping himself in a stony coat of indomitable
resolve. The unstoppable object going through the immovable
barrier, with all that terrible English stubbornness, that beef-
steak John Bull tenacity that carried the Union Jack up Gibral-
tar and across Nyasaland and planted it atop Mount Everest to
make heaven and hell protectorates, I suppose. Neither of us
mentioned Jones. We barely spoke. Once Smythe curtly told
me I could go back, but he would carry on.

You know why I stuck, and it wasn't bravery. All heads aside,
that country would have scared my teeth to clattering; added
the new disaster of Captain Jones (the man had been swallowed
as completely as Bellweather) and my blood cooled to icewater.
It wasn't courage that kept my horse on that path. No! It was
the thought of that rotten Little Dog with its diamond tongue
which held me to the trail. That diamond tongue shimmering

before my eyes in a constant mirage, a growing delusion that was gripping me like a drug.

I'd thought of nothing else from the moment I'd seen those subconscious sketchings in Bellweather's book; and I'm trying to tell you it wasn't any righteous desire to avenge those awful murders, it wasn't fortitude or intent to aid the Law that had me following the Union Jack to the carnivorous heart of Bhutan.

We cantered at dusty noon through a crenellated mud wall into that mountain-clutched town, and I think I know how the French Royalists felt in the tumbrils. Built Tibetan fashion, the place sprawled uphill in hive-like tiers; the natives swarmed out at us like hungry bees. Those Bhutanese devils knew we were coming. Their drums had probably been telegraphing the word from the moment we crossed their border, and they gave us a reception that frizzled my hair.

WE WEREN'T through the gate before the outer walls were picketed with shaggy, Mongol-cheeked barbarians, fierce as hawks, each one grinning behind a long-barreled jezail. Dogs, crones, urchins and lepers hollered from every mud door. I think the welcoming committee would have terrorized a regiment of Bengal Lancers.

First came a dwarf leading a moulting yak with a veiled holy man perched up top like a monkey on a mastodon. A ballet of half-naked *dombers* followed, a score of whooping jugglers in devil masks, dancing and spinning under colored umbrellas, whirling bone rattles and gesturing like the inmates of a madhouse. Then a squad of mounted guerillas pounding on huge wooden kettledrums, and finally a crew of bald-shaved, yellow-robed priests.

Baying, caterwauling, drumming, tooting, this merrymaking mob surrounded our horses and drowned us under an oratorio of sound, thunderous and impressive as a Bach Magnificat. Every man and boy in that benighted stronghold carried a butcher knife or a scimitar; and you can visualize the two of us, ragged and dirty as old towels, saddle-worn, ashen from want of sleep, a couple of gray scarecrows caught in the middle of that carnival.

My throat ached with fear, but Major Smythe showed no dismay. In that swirl of dust, stench and din he sat his saddle like Wellington after Waterloo, and bawled a demand to see the Rajah. The high priest on the yak seemed only too willing to grant the request, beckoning us forward with a spider's smile; and my heart sank to my boots when we pulled up before a sort of stockade, marched across a stony compound and entered a domed building of rose-colored stone that looked and smelled first cousin to an invaded tomb.

Myself, I'd anticipated a sort of Taj Mahal palace with swimming pools of perfume, marble corridors, secret harems and cobra-like music in the wings. One of those collegiate Rajahs owning a fraternity pin, an exquisite taste in poetry and women, a connoisseur of emeralds and torture instruments. Jeweled turban and silk bloomer, crosslegged on a peacock throne. This Bhutanese specimen was something else again. Afterwards I found out there are two Rajahs in Bhutan; one who has charge of the governing end of the business, another who has charge of the spiritual. I'm sure we interviewed the fellow who had charge of the spiritual.

A pair of yellow-skinned doormen salaamed all over the place and politely requested our armaments. I had a heart-sink, and looked at Smythe for advice. Cool as a salad, the British officer unhooked his gun belt and passed it to the check room. Not being corseted in that whalebone British confidence, I suffered a qualm at handing over my Lüger, and the qualm continued as I followed Smythe's cavalry boots into a room as stark as a lamasery crypt, a prison-walled chamber illuminated by narrow barred windows and the beard of the old man sitting his heels in the center of the floor.

That beard seemed to take up half the room. It drank up the light and sent it back in wave-rays of silver. It covered its owner like a fall of snow, his hands sticking out through this hairy cataract like brown gloves reaching from a frozen fountain. Saucery black eyes and gnomish bald head peeped over the crest of this glacier. Methuselah? Well, how could that Oriental have raised such foliage in less than a thousand years? Talk about the Old Man of the Mountain!

AND THIS was the head Rajah of Bhutan, ace pilot of the country's one-ship air corps! I tell you, it gave me a shock. Smythe inhaled a "Bloody!" then pulled upright with a jerk. The man had stuffing, all right.

It was something to see him adjust his helmet strap, set his shoulders, clap his heels and face that Wizard of Oz with all the assurance of a general about to dress down an insubordinate subadar. He mentioned His Britannic Majesty and the Emperor of India as if they were standing behind him; cut the preamble in the bud, and got right down to brass tacks.

"I want to know what you've done with Captain Jones!"

I was supposed to play interpreter and relay the ultimatum in Bhutanese, but before I could think up the idiom, a pink mouth opened in the frosty beard and the Rajah answered in English.

"By what authority does my visitor address me, Exalted ruler of Bhutan, in tones of command?" A brown hand petted the snow under a now visible lower lip. The eyes blinked. "The Deputy Commissioner *Sahib* is doubtless aware a gesture from me could easily extinguish his life."

If Smythe wasn't aware of it, I was. Double doubtless! I could feel the color running out of my face and throat, and I cursed myself for being there. Not so my companion! Right then I think the man could have bluffed Saint Peter into an admission that the Gates were stolen from London Tower and King George was very anxious to get them back.

"The Rajah of Bhutan," he suggested sternly, "is also doubtless aware that two of my policemen have carried to Gaugtok word of my intention to visit you here. Should I fail to return to India the British *Raj* would crush the Exalted ruler of Bhutan as the foot of the elephant crushes the toad. Even now the uncounted soldiers of the Viceroy are gathered on your borders, awaiting my safe conduct."

It was almost convincing. The black eyes filled with a concilia-tory humility, almost convincing too. "You come seeking some-one, then? A white *Sahib* lost in my kingdom?"

"I demand to know what you've done with the police captain stolen from our camp five days' march to the south," Smythe blazed. "I demand information on the murder of the Sikh lieu-tenant, Abdurahman, also ambushed and slain thereabouts. There is also the matter of the American *shikari* lately murdered in the hills, and the five *Feringi* whose heads were sent to Gaug-tok by airplane and flung in that river as mud at my police!"

I WISH you could have seen the eyes in that hairy halo in midroom. Innocence? Saucers of India ink. That archaic patri-arch could wring more expression from his pupils than the Divine Sarah from her whole face. "Airplane?" He wheezed the difficult word. "Airship? Ahee, my masters, but this man-made bird of the sky has long been unable to flap its wings at the magi-cal command of its wheels. Look then from yonder window and see this truth."

I know some of the bluff came out of Smythe at that little disclosure. I heard it gag through his windpipe. Yonder window was there, all right, just beyond the ancient's pointed finger; and just beyond the frame of the window we could see a patch of stony compound and something piled up on the rocks like a heap of old bones. Told what to look for, I was able to distinguish the jagged blade of a smashed propeller, splintered framework and rusted engine parts, the whole overgrown by a thicket of burrs and weeds. It was the Rajah's toy for a fact, and it must have been cracked up in the latter days of the War.

And the pilot who washed the bottom out of that early flying machine, washed the bottom out of Deputy Commissioner Smythe's hydra-headed murder case. I could see his theory of those air-mailed heads piling up in a similar crash under his scalp. Bewilderment, consternation, something close to alarm twisted across his features, screwed together, exploded into a bomb-burst wrath.

"By heaven, then," he thundered, whirling on Whitebeard, "how'd you send those heads to Gaugtok? Where's the fiend who cut them off—"

A forthright man, Major Smythe, and he got a forthright answer from Whitebeard. "The fiend who cut them off," the great eyes saddened dolorously, "is everywhere."

"Who is he?" Smythe screamed. "Tell me what you mean, you triple-tongued old hamadryad, or I'll wring your own head off those lying whiskers—"

"His name," our informant murmured, "is Greed."

"Greed?" I can tell you the Deputy Commissioner was losing temper fast. He'd come through hell on a murder trail, and his patience was too short for this sort of folderol. His hand threatened into a fist, but the grandfather of Socrates holding the middle of the floor didn't wink a lash.

"Ai, Greed," he said in a voice hollow as a sermon, "for I think the men you seek, those who lost the heads from their bodies, came here lusting for that which was forbidden to man. Forget not the sublime Eightfold Path to Karma, the voice of the Gautama saying, 'Among men who are greedy let us dwell free from greed.' Heed well the warning of Buddha, saying, 'Beware lest thine avarice trip thee.' Hear the lesson of the Little Dog!"

Before we could stop him he was telling us the story of the Little Dog, and after he got it started we couldn't have stopped him if we'd wanted to. Substantially it was the same old dog story, yet I couldn't begin to tell it the way he told it, not on your life. It wasn't what he said, but the way he said it. He threw his hands and his eyes and his whiskers into that little parable, and what he couldn't do with the voice box buried in his beard just wasn't worth doing. That Rajah of Punaka could preach! The words came rolling out of his whiskers like thunder out of clouds while his eyes played lightning above the storm. My, how he handled that parable! That old Snow Man took the bedtime story and made it into a *Marseillaise,* a Disraeli oration, a Cross of Gold speech.

He made Buddha and his pet come strolling out of the glooms in front of us. He made us see that ten-foot dog with its golden body, its diamond tongue. We saw it close its merry eyes in a nap under the giant *bo* tree; we saw the bandits creeping up; heard the twanging arrows and crashing rocks, the snap of that breaking hind leg, the roar of laughter as the injured animal awoke and bit the head from its tripped-up assailant—ha, ha, ha!

Our nerves were catgut strings, and that ancient story-teller played on us as if we were a couple of old violins. I let out a groan when he described the size and luster of the diamond mouthpiece, and the pair of us yelled like fools when the bandits were getting scalped. We forgot why we were in that one-room palace in the heart of Bhutan. We forgot about Jones and Abdurahman and Bellweather and those others, listening to the voice of Buddha casting his curse on avaricious mankind. It was a great sermon! Another hour of that old man's preaching and I'd have hit the sawdust trail as a Llamaist, I give you my word. I looked at the Deputy Commissioner and saw him sweating harder than a bottle of cold champagne.

THEN OLD Man Methuselah brought us smack into the present with a jump. "The lesson of the master holds true to this day," he snored. "Beware of the Little Dog, lest your greed betray your feet and the diamond tongue should laugh. He who hears the laughter of the Little Dog shall lose the head from his body; and his victims are many. The Little Dog knows. Visit him with stealth and lust in your heart and you trip of it and die, even as those you sought here have died—"

The domed room was filled with a mulberry twilight when the sermon was over, the Rajah giving a little signal to show he'd finished his testimony. There was a harsh sound of Smythe breathing. A struggle was taking place under the British officer's khaki sun helmet, a mental scrap that jutted a vein on his forehead. British agnosticism fighting with mystic conjurations of the old saga-singer's voice.

"You aren't trying to tell me the Little Dog *is* in Bhutan!"

"Where Buddha left him, my masters. Sitting under the tree."

Smythe's teeth looked dry, spitting, "Bah! You've murdered those travelers in cold blood, and you're trying to stall us with a wonderful fairy story. You think to cheat the British *Raj* with such tommyrot?"

"To see," the white beard reminded us, "is to believe."

The policeman had to laugh, a sound as husky as the rattle of dry nipa fronds in an arid wind. "You confounded old *fakir*, you mean to pretend we can see this golden dog of Buddha's with its diamond tongue—"

The Rajah of Bhutan stood up in his beard. An arm like a shinbone came out through the waterfall whiskers, the saucer eyes shone like polished black stones at the crest of a miniature Victoria Nyanza, a finger jabbed in gloom. "Go thou unmolested and see. Follow the cañon beyond the western gate and three days into the south. There stands the sacred mountain and the giant tree in the sky. There sits the Little Dog. You will see the golden hide; the shine of the tongue that is of a thousand suns. See, my masters, and believe—"

CHAPTER IV

"IT'S REAL!"

WELL, THE SMELL of the Little Dog was so strong in the air by that time that I never smelled any rat. Something in the Rajah's rendition of Buddha's gospel convinced me an image was there for the seeing, and my temperature was up a hundred degrees.

Smythe's cheekbones looked shiny and feverish, too. His airplane theory was a pile of kindling out there in the Rajah's compound. He couldn't arrest this Himalayan beglerbeg, invading Bhutan as he had without authority; if he lifted a finger toward that patriarch every man jack in the stronghold would have jumped us and chopped us to mince. Under the circumstances there wasn't much of an alternative.

"Come on, Bradshaw," he jerked at me, "we'll investigate this idolatrous balderdash. And if there isn't any Little Dog there," with a glare at our host, "I'll have the lancers up here to smoke out these head-hunters to the last pig. We'll blow up this Little Dog alibi right now!"

We rode out of town with the drums and cowhorns bedlamming behind us, and I think we were both a little mad when we found the cañon beyond the western gate and started south down the trail. I know I was. Our punitive expedition had become a hodgepodge of Scotland Yard, Houdini disappearances and Arabian Nights that had my brain out of cog. A British cop starts out to capture an Asian homicidal maniac, and is told the killer's name is Greed. Typical of the East to answer the

West with an allegory, but no allegory could dump five heads in a river behind a police station, decapitate an American big game hunter and a Sikh policeman within a fortnight, or kidnap a Tommy captain out from under your nose.

"There's just a chance," Smythe said behind his teeth. "Just a chance—"

"Chance of what?" I wanted to know. A chance of finding poor Jones alive? I had an idea Smythe might be planning a sneak back into the stronghold at midnight, and the idea made me sick. I told myself Jones was dead. I told myself it was suicidal for us to pester the Rajah further. But away down deep inside, I knew I wanted to rush off in search of that golden-flanked, diamond-tongued dog. That is what makes me sick now. To remember how all that time my mind was on a treasure. The deaths of those others meant nothing. My own head meant nothing. I could only think of a diamond as big as ten Kizam Stars with a shine to rival a thousand suns. I could think of nothing but a million dollars.

"The gem is still there in the image," I mentally figured. "The natives haven't stolen it because the idol is sacred and they're scared of Buddha's curse. Bellweather and the rest came hunting the thing, and the priests killed them. But Smythe's threat about the Indian Army has bluffed them down. They won't dare touch us."

You see how it was? I didn't dare hunt for Jones', but I wasn't afraid to go after that holy bonanza. If Smythe had any plans of police work, he didn't confide them. He gave no answer to my query, nor did he propose to turn about. We walked our horses to the cañon's bend, and when we reached the place where we were lost from sight of the town, the Deputy Commissioner slammed the spurs into his mount. Go! Down the trail he dashed like a Cossack, I after him.

FROM THAT spurt forward, we rode like a pair of jockeys trying to win the Calcutta sweepstakes. I feel sorry for our horses when I remember that cañon trail. It was a terrible trail. We rode those poor animals to skeletons, and anything but an Indian pony would have dropped under such punishment.

The path petered out into an obstacle race of bramble thickets and rocks; daytime the cañon bottom was either gushing rainwater or steam, after sundown it was choked with the darkness of an anthracite shaft. Now Smythe cursed and raved at the slightest delay, squirming at every dismount, bolting the rations from his saddle bag, dithering to be off. Nights we flopped from the saddle, hobbled the ponies, then fell to the weeds around a campfire and lay in sore exhaustion.

Have you ever been too tired to sleep? Well, after three days and nights of that kind of steeplechase I was so fatigued by insomnia I lost balance the minute my boot touched ground. I lay wide awake in the wire-grass and mud, every bone throbbing like a tooth, my eyes sticking out of their sockets, staring at hallucinary visions of Buddha's dog. It would be there. It had to be there. Bellweather had known about it, and the Rajah had told the truth.

I could see the Deputy Commissioner hugging the fire, Webley on knee, nervously twisting his glance this way and that at the encroaching shadows. We must be pretty close to the spot where the Rajah promised we'd find the mountain and the tree, but the clouds had blotted out the cañon tops since afternoon; in the turgid and soggy blackness, the close, skyless night, you couldn't see a star. Lord, wasn't it dark! Our handful of firelight touched the creeper-wrapped trunk of a *sal* tree a few paces distant and came running back for comfort near the coals.

In the flame-glow Smythe was gaunt. These last three days he had shed a lot of his beef. His jutting cheekbones, more prominent than before, took on the febrile glow of the blaze; his eyes tinged unnatural red. Dirty blue stubble bristled on his jaws, and when an Englishman won't take time out to shave you can bet your life something's wrong. I wondered if he was afraid we were being followed by a secret detachment of Bhutanese butcher boys carrying special instructions. Smythe didn't say. For the past fifty hours he'd scarcely spoken anything but oaths.

Myself, I didn't believe there was a native within leagues of the cañon. Our mounts might have broken a trail that hadn't been trod since the Primal Day. I was certain no skulking humans were ambushed ahead of us because of another peril which had thickened with every southward mile. Tigers! In that mountain corridor the spoor was everywhere, and that very afternoon I'd spied at least five of the brutes skedaddling away in the underbrush. Signs of a whole flock of tigers, and pretty good evidence there weren't any natives about. Tigers or head-hunters, you can take your pick. All in all, I fell asleep that night with the feel of more than danger tickling at my scalp.

I HEARD Smythe saying, "I'll guard the horses till midnight, then you can spell me off," and I must have slipped asleep right afterwards. At any rate I was chilled stiff when I next came to what was left of my senses, lurching upright in the night-drenched grass.

At first I thought I'd winked off hardly a minute, and then I realized I must have snored several hours. A single coal remained of the campfire, but the cañon was filled with a luminous silver radiance, blue on rock and grass, black in shadow, night-lit by a great mid-summer moon. Only a gauzy scarf of cloud clinging to the moon's saffron shoulder remained of the thunderheads. The sky was clean to the stars, and the cañon walls stood up in clear-cut black silhouette. How still it was in that lunar scene! Draining foliage, the twittering of tree frogs, magnified the quiet by a thousand. It was too quiet. My skin itched suddenly, and I tossed a hand to my gun butt.

"Smythe!" I yipped.

One of the horses snorted. The shadow I'd addressed as the Deputy Commissioner was a tree. Deputy Commissioner, Major Colin Smythe wasn't there. Deputy Commissioner, Major Colin Smythe wasn't anywhere.

Yanking my automatic, I reached my feet in the same frightened reflex. "Smythe!" I muted the yell, and it wasn't loud enough. No answer. Silence, moonlight, and me, alone in that cañon bottom. There are plenty of times when I like to be by myself, but this wasn't one of them. It put a strain on my gregarious instinct that amounted to a panic. I sent my eyes around the camp, off through shadows, leaping over rocks and up the cañon walls in a stricken hunt for companionship that didn't flush a rupee's worth. Smythe had gone with the clouds. Absorbed in the Asian moonlight? Or the elves had taken him away. Shaggy Bhutanese elves carrying butcher knives to belt, and special instructions from the home office!

Am I telling this with too much restraint? Well, I was so splendidly gibbered that my gullet turned to an icicle in my neck, the gun shook out of my fingers, and I had to pick it out of the grass; and I'd have stampeded down the cañon howling and firing if I hadn't seen something else just then. Printed against the sky across the cañon. Clear in moonlight atop the tallest crag. Towering above the forest-wigs below. A giant *bo* tree!

CAN YOU see me shin-banging across that cañon bottom as if the brains were out of my head? Plunging in and out of thickets like a swimmer tearing through surf? Galloping across rocks, clawing holes through jungle, fighting my way up that cliff like a human fly going up your Flat-iron Building? The trail wasn't hard to navigate with that tree up there like the North Star. Just hard enough to slash the knees from my breeches, bloody the nails on my fingers and stab a few thorns in my hands.

Finally there was something like a path, and I wasn't too tired to run it, either, or too scared to chase it along a chasm-rim that dropped sheer below like a look from a balloon. Five miles? Ten? I don't know. But the moon was up in the tree when I got there, and under it—well, I broke from the jungle's fringe into open ground and froze colder than a frog before a crocodile. Every time I think of how I charged into that mountain-top glade it sends ice beads down my spine, and once again I can whiff that smell. The smell of the Little Dog!

YOU'VE SMELLED age? Did you ever get a whiff of something that was fashioned when the world was young? You get the same sort of noseful when you walk inside an Egyptian pyramid or saunter down into one of those newly-excavated temples at Ankor. Well, that grandfather of all *bo* trees must have been a seedling around the time Buddha decided to leave the wife and kiddies and start a religion, and the dog crouching in the shadow of the tree must have been a pup in the sculptor's studio while the steam was still cooling on the Himalayas.

Rajah of Bhutan

Asia can stack up more mysteries per square mile than the other continents lumped together, and how that colossal image came atop this God-forgotten mountain in Bhutan was a mystery of the highest altitude. I know that glade wasn't far from the timber line. The dog sat in the middle of a clearing, and the clearing sat in the middle of one of those blanks on the atlas marked "Unexplored." Think of a mastiff thirty feet long, five feet from belly to back-arch, *couchant* on a slab of granite, head on paws, eyes staring, tail curled up over the haunches, alert as life and ready to pounce. Picture it made of gold. Metal shining yellow like one of those tub-butter carvings you see in restaurant windows. Buddha and no man living could have lifted the thing. It must have weighed tons.

I'll never see a bit of sculpting like that again. It was crude, badly proportioned, all scrawled over with scrolls and curlicues, but the image had more life than I did at that moment. The master who modeled it had imagination. Gold arrows were sticking in all directions from the gold dog's ribs, and, what was more, the left hind leg had been cracked off at the hip and lay alongside in the weeds. Remember the parable? Well, Buddha's pet was meeting all the requirements of the story. All the requirements! When I tell you this gold hound's mouth was open, jaws apart, carved teeth gleaming—wide open on a yawn like an open window and about as big—you may believe. But you may not believe what was inside that mouth.

You could see a dark throat dropping into the dog's interior, all right, and deep at the back of the mouth, big as a brick—Lord! I wish you could have seen it with the moonbeams flaming in and out in restive fire, the sapphire twinkle and blaze, a thousand carved facets shimmering, glittering, gleaming rainbow colors, lighting the dog's palate like a sunburst. The diamond tongue!

A million arrows of livid, multicolored fire sprinkled out of the beastly image's mouth and hit me in the eyes. Man, it lit up the whole place! If you could have seen that image under that tree with the moon pouring in and out of its jaws, the jungle-thick silence walling around, you would know my sensations on the edge of that shrine!

A walkway of thick paving blocks led straight up to the idol's opened mouth, and I stood at the walkway's end, leering like a drunkard. There wasn't a sound. There wasn't a sound for miles. The smell of antiquity, the shine of that thing in the image's mouth, the wilderness silence paralyzed me. And then—like a phantom merging into focus it was—I saw something else.

A living head crouched in the weeds not four paces from the dog's rump. Two scarlet-rimmed eyeballs peeping. The faint gleam of parted teeth. He wasn't looking at me. He didn't see me. He'd made a sortie around that tree to be sure everything was all right, a little scouting tour to reconnoiter the lay-out, and now he was crawling to the fore the way those fairy tale brigands crawled when they made their attack in the legend. If the eyes of the image glared, you should have seen the eyeballs behind these beet-veined lids. Never have I seen such eyes! His features were scribbled, screwed, wrenched almost beyond recognition.

It was Deputy Commissioner Smythe.

"It's real!" he was panting.

CHAPTER V

THE LITTLE DOG LAUGHS

WELL, IF IT was, it was the only reality in that aberrant minute; the gulp wasn't out of the Deputy Commissioner's mouth when some magnetic impulse (I hadn't made a sound) turned him in the weeds and those railway signal eyes looked straight at me.

"Bradshaw!" he screamed, leaping up like a piston, hip deep in the brush. His head, patterned in moonlight, seemed to swell, suffused. Zip! His gun was out before I could ask why. I can see him in my dreams standing there near that idolatrous tree, near that festive dog, his features bulged, pointing that shining Webley automatic straight at me, finger snatching on the trigger.

I stood like a cigar store Comanche, stunned to wood by the thing. The Deputy Commissioner was shooting at me. At me! *Tchickety-tchik! Tchickety-tchik!* The sound of that trigger wakes me sweating out of sleep to this day. Clicking like a sewing machine. For perhaps twelve awful seconds that was the only sound; then I shocked out of trance with a gasp, whipped up my Lüger and returned the man's fire, shot for shot. *Clickety-click-ety-click!* Lord, what a duel that was! It must have lasted fully a minute; and we weren't eight paces apart, the Englishman and I, triggering away like fools, not a sound, not a flash, not a smoke-burst, not a bullet in the moonlight.

I didn't know then, but I realize now what had happened. Why our guns didn't fire, I mean. We'd parked them at the palace door up there in Punaka, and while we were inside confabing with the Rajah his smart doormen had emptied the magazines. Those pilfering Bhutanese had saved my life, too. The Deputy Commissioner would have shot me to sponge on the first blast. I wasn't long in finding out why. Empty gun still chattering in his fist, he came charging across the moonpath at me like a maddened rhino.

"You shan't have the diamond! It's mine! Mine—"

His face was wrinkled and liverish. Green eyes aslant, lips stretched over gnashed teeth, head down, arms flailing, he hit me like a catapult, striking and screaming as he struck. *Crack!* "All the years I've spent in that filthy frontier station—"— *Crack!*—"Lifetime in that tuppence policeman's job!"—*Crack!*— "Heat! Dirt! Beastly rotten food. I'm not going back to it, I tell you. Scrimping and blistering! King and country! Bah! All my life in that stinking little outpost for nothing—"—*Crack!*—"I saw the Little Dog first! You shan't have any of it! It's mine!"

He struck me a half dozen times before I could lift a finger; the moonshine turned to vapor before my eyes and every blow of that gun raining down on my scalp, jaws, shoulders, was a hammer driving his screams like spikes through my brain. I saw a terrible thing through those stars. I saw a man's soul go to pieces. I saw a man's soul go rotten as the features of Jekyll went rotten when he drank the poison and changed into Hyde.

The Little Dog's tongue was the poison. That diamond had been on Smythe's mind, too, and his murderer hunt to Punaka had spoiled into a treasure hunt. Before the blaze of that terrible gem his British decorum peeled off him like so much sunburn. Propriety, discipline, all that English training and johnny sportsmanship scabbed away like varnish from wormwood. The sight of that bonanza blazing within reach had knocked his civilization galley west; he'd have shot me down in cold blood; he was trying to kill me—

"You shan't have it," he kept screeching. "It's all mine—"

I SMASHED at his mouth with my Lüger, and we went into a spinning adagio. No Marquis of Queensberry rules. Punching and sledging toe to toe with iron-filled fists. Bodies colliding, threshing together, kicking, beating, cursing, gouging. We fell, rolled across the ground tearing the weeds, uprooting brushwood. I had to fight for my life. The man was battering me blind, and I punched my gun muzzle under his chin and cracked the head back on his neck. Slamming a knee into my stomach, he forced me to earth and put the ball of his thumb into my eye, and in that torture I dropped my Lüger, lost it among the weeds. I could hear him squawking like a parrot, then, and I caught him in an arm lock that altered his voice to a shriek. With a sudden wrench I flopped him corkscrew and kicked his Webley flying.

Somehow we were on our feet, and didn't he battle! The man could slug. *Thud! Thwack!* Trading blows that echoed off through the jungle like the sound of a woodsman's ax. I guess they train those Britishers to box. I whaled at him with everything I had, and my fists bounced from his jawbone with no more effect than cotton balls. He drove my shins out from under me with a rugby player's kick, hitting me as I staggered and spun.

"You shan't have the diamond! You shan't have any of it—"

Howling the words in a sort of refrain he began to chop me down ruthlessly, systematically, a jab under the heart, a driving uppercut, a cross to the side of the head. The sight of his face took the heart out of me. I was sick. My untimed blows, skidding when they struck, bothered him no more than slaps. His lower lip was cut and hanging, his face empurpled, but I couldn't put out the green lights of his eyes nor stop his trampling, pounding charges that were beating me to the ground.

Jackets ripped at collar and elbow, faces spurting, fists churning, lungs chugging gasps of aged wind, the moon on us like a stage spot, the valley swimming in silver far below—was there ever such a prize ring or such an audience? Can you picture us fighting before that open-mouthed watchdog on its pedestal under the ancient tree? I could see it following our gladiatorial show with its heathenish statue eyes, its wide mouth grinning, soundless mirth yapping from that dazzling tongue. What a laugh it must have had when the berserk police officer hammered me to my knees under a blizzard of fists, clutched a grip on my throat and flung me throttled under his knee.

"Now, damn you," he was gulping like an opened whisky bottle, wheezing and breathless from the homicidal efforts of his fingers, "now you're through. I'll kill you. Oh ho! They won't find you, either, m'lad. There's th' tigers—" his hands tightened on my windpipe with the power of a tourniquet, "there's th' tigers to carry your carcass off, and me—ha!—who's to stop me? Who's to stop me once I get my hands on that gem? It's mine, d'you hear? Who's to stop me once I own that fortune? Paris! London! Anywhere I want. Rich. They'll make me a bloody lordship—me!—get me out of India—*Sir* Colin, they'll say—*Sir!*—"

HE WAS banging my skull on the ground so hard the whole mountain seemed to shake. Strangling me with the power of a madman. I don't think the man's brain had spoiled, but his soul had gone mad, you understand. His heel-clicking, routine pinch-penny, police official soul had curdled to fust at the sight of that million-karat sparkler and the thought of what it would buy for him. He was a devil, and on my word, he was killing me!

The feeling was pounded out of my skull and my skin went numb. Mountain, jungle, the moon in the treetop, the Little Dog and the Deputy Commissioner went merry-go-round before my puffed eyeballs. Blackness was drowning me. Dust and leaf mold plugged my nostrils, my heart was bursting, I could hear my head whacking ground louder than a door-knocker, but I couldn't throw him off or stop it. His green eyes grew and grew in the darkness, gloating on my destruction. God knows what instinct pulled the trick that saved my life.

It wasn't play acting when my body went limp and my arms quit work and hung. I must have been black with suffocation. But I did turn the eyes up in my head and loosen my tongue, and when his fingers let go and he sprang to his feet, I lay playing dead for all I was worth, hardly daring to swallow a breath. Only a couple of ticks left in my heart, believe you me, and I nursed them along and played corpse without much pretense. Another squeeze on the throat would have finished me.

Smythe was convinced. He shrugged and backed away, dusting off his hands, whining and whispering under his breath, his head turned toward the image as if expecting from the thing a word of approval. The yawning gem-glow came like witchshine across the glade and put a rainbow on the man's knotted forehead. He lifted a hand as if to shade the glimmer from his face. His shoulders sloped. His torn under-lip closed up over his mouth, touching his nose. He snorted a breath, wheeled, started at the idol on the run.

Often since, I've heard the clack of his spurred leather heels sprinting up the flagstone walkway toward the giant tree. Lying on my side in a paralysis stiffer than a wax Crusader on a coffin in Westminster, I saw him charge up the path toward that golden idol, hands stretched to grab for the gem. I'm sure he was grinning. I know the Little Dog was. And as long as I live I'll never eradicate from memory that picture. *Whack! Clang!* It happened and was over with all the speed and unsuspected violence of a mousetrap.

Smythe wasn't a yard from the image, legs pumping along a gentle downgrade, when he fell kerwhack—tripped on his own greed, for all you could see of what had caught his ankles and sent him plunging. On my honor, it was exactly as if he'd been thrown by a moonbeam. His feet were snatched out from under him, swish! and in that second a magical spider-thread of light shivered across his stumbled boots and I heard him howl as if his shins had cracked on a curbstone.

CLEAN AS a halfback tackled within reach of the goal posts, Smythe spilled headlong in his tracks, but he didn't hit the pavement. You know he didn't! Some master calculator had measured the arc of such a fall, and figured it to perfection. Only a man of height less than average—a German airman named Lunt, for example—would have fallen short of the mark. Deputy Commissioner, Major Colin Smythe had been made to measure for the job. Pitching bodily toward the Little Dog, his head fell squarely and truly into the yawning, diamond-lit mouth and that gold lower jaw caught him exactly under the chin. *Whack!*

And *clang!* A fluid explosion in the moonlight. Crimson showering the air. A scarlet streak that landed like tobacco juice clear to where I lay and smacked my shirtfront. The screech that came out of me lifted me upright and standing. I won't forget that minute till my dying day. It wasn't my dying day right then, but it was Smythe's. I saw him rotate on a side-wise spin; saw him stagger and whirl, arms outflung, legs tangling, crashing off into the gladeside weeds for a place to fall, and where his head had been—

Snapped by some deadly spring-lever hidden in its mouth, the golden jaws of the Little Dog had smashed together with the clang of a lion-trap. One bite! Knives for teeth. In one yellow flash the jaws slammed shut, in another they sprang open, and that was all. The Little Dog was quiet under his tree. Eyes staring. Head on paws. Mouth a-yawn, throat empty at one swallow, diamond tongue winkering and shimmering and more like a ruby, just then, you may take my word! And where Smythe's head had been there wasn't any head. His head was gone in one gulp!

I stared at the terrible image with its shark-open mouth and illuminated gullet, and I guess there wasn't much left of my own head either. I said that idol's jaws had smashed shut and that was all. Well, it wasn't. Just as Smythe's face plunged into that golden maw, on the moment those jaws bit down, I heard a laugh. It wasn't any human laugh. A cavernous, rumbling bellylaugh, it was—a booming, echoy, wind-blown gurgling roar that burst from the idol's throat in one belching guffaw like the drunkard mirth of hell's doors blown open to receive a newcomer. *Blob-blobble-blaaah!* No, I didn't imagine it. It echoed down the valley into faint sounds of watery thunder, coming from the Little Dog's mouth in a gust as freezing as a breath from the Poles, icing my cheek, shaking the jungle leaves behind me. And in that one dreadful swallow it was gone.

I got away from that shrine. Ran half way down the mountain and fell the rest. All through the night, all through ensuing uncountable days I rode out of Bhutan as if the legions of Eblis were after me; and the army doctor in Gaugtok told me I was the worst case of brain fever he'd had in years.

EPILOGUE

BRADSHAW'S VOICE CHOKED off into grim-lipped quiet, and the only sound on his veranda was the murmur of insects crowding the screen and the far, clear tinkle of a temple bell in the moon-laved native city below. The fat-legged New York broker, the tea planter and I sat staring. The naturalist stared with us but not at us, his hardened gaze on the distant caravan of Himalayan peaks shadowmarching eastward.

"Well," came his conclusion in a flattened husk, "that's why I don't like hyenas or any other kind of laughing dog. They remind me of that image up there in Bhutan. They remind me of Smythe's degeneration when he saw that laughing tongue, that wonderful bonanza, and lost his head over the thing. Worst of all, I'm reminded it might have been *my* head, instead, for I wasn't a bit less greedy than the others. Stroon, the Dutch silk buyer. Sir Enoch, the geographer. Grusbaum the gem merchant, and Lunt the little airman who fell short on the trip-up and caught it just under the ears."

The naturalist twisted in his chair. "Each of those fellows had gone up there to grab the diamond. They entered Bhutan by roundabout trails, faking disappearances to put anybody who might follow them off the track. They wanted to find the Little Dog and have it all by themselves when they found it. Same as Bellweather. He must have spotted the big tree on the skyline from our camp which, I afterwards discovered, was just the other side of the mountain, the next valley beyond the cañon where

Smythe and I ended up. Bellweather spied the tree and hiked off by himself because he wanted the diamond whole-hog. So did Abdurahman when he was left up there to stand guard. And that's what happened to Jones. The Little Dog got them all. It would have laughed my head off, too, if Smythe hadn't been there to grab first. I, too, would have stumbled on my greed—"

The tea planter made a sound of protest. "It's a charming allegory," he complained, "but I don't quite get it. I mean, this business about being tripped up by greed and all that. What I mean to say is, this blighter Smythe went headlong so literally. Doesn't it seem—er—a bit on the longbow side that the fellow should have stumbled so neatly at just the precise moment?"

Bradshaw gave us a salty smile. "As a kid I used to rig up a trick somewhat on the same order. You know small-town boys. We'd tie a long thread to a couple of tin cans and stretch the thread across the sidewalk in the shadow of an elm. Then the minister would come along and get the thread caught in his gaiters, jerking the cans in a great clatter up the pavement. I'd never have dreamed the trick had come from the hills of Asia."

"You mean," the planter gasped, "Smythe fell over a thread?"

"A silver wire," the naturalist explained. "A wire so fine you could hardly see it with the naked eye, and you'd never see it with your eye on that sparkler in the idol's mouth. Long ago the Orient knew the secret of making a delicate metal thread, and only an Asian priest could have rigged it up. Tight as a mandolin string, and it was stretched ankle-high across the walkway leading to the image under the *bo* tree, and that cunning thread would have thrown a ton. I suppose it was strung by the engineers who set up the Little Dog, and only God knows the number who defied Buddha's parable and ran to grab the decoying diamond, went tripping kerflop—"

"But say," the planter persisted, "how'd the heads get back to Gaugtok like you said? Who rushed them down into India from Bhutan and chucked them into the river behind the police station, there?"

BRADSHAW HAD to clear harshness from his throat before replying. "Nobody took 'em there. To begin with, I told you that mountainside was infested with tigers. That's why we didn't find any bodies around the shrine to warn us away. Place was a feeding ground for the tigers and they'd drag the bodies off. The Little Dog's laughter took care of the heads. The image was hollow and the throat went down like a well. I'll bet it went down a mile. When the metal jaws were sprung, a trap opened in the throat, and the laughter I heard was the sound of an underground river that was rushing through the bottoms of that mountain range. That was the laughter, and that's how those heads got into the stream that bubbled from the rocks behind Gaugtok. There were seven heads on the table when I got back to that town. Jones's and Smythe's. And when I think of how near the Little Dog came to having the laugh on *me*—"

It was the New Yorker who interrupted this time. The fat man was on his feet, jellied with excitement. "You're not telling us you left that treasure up there, are you? A gold image like that? And the diamond! Why, man, if it's still *up* there—say, I don't *have* to be back in New York until—"

The broker's eyes were big as poppies. He didn't see the look Bradshaw gave him; didn't notice the naturalist was gone from his chair, indoors and back, until he caught the shimmer of something in Bradshaw's hand. Then the fat New Yorker gave a yell. So did the planter and I. Light ricocheted from the object in the naturalist's fingers, twinkled and arrowed at our eyes, put a rainbow on the broker's forehead.

"I went back there, myself," Bradshaw was saying. "You see, I hadn't had enough. I jumped the silver wire and smashed the trap jaw with an ax. I blew the image to pieces with a charge of dynamite, and I got its tongue. And he had the last laugh, that Little Dog. I guess this tongue is laughing yet. I staked my shirt to go back and steal this thing, but you can't get around the wisdom of Buddha with all your modern craft. The dog was made of iron and gold paint. This diamond is a swell lump of glass." He gave the broker a meaningful chuckle. "It looks like a million, doesn't it? And it's worth no more than those stocks you're rushing back to buy."

ABOUT THE AUTHOR

AS A GUEST speaker at Pulpcon in Dayton, Ohio in July, 1986, I played the old Q. and A. game. I believe the opening of that game makes a good beginning for the present discussion of my fiction writing for the pulps.

Q. How and when did my fiction writing begin?

A. I have in my files the initial effort—a book entitled *The Devul and the Knight* [sic] written age five, hand-printed, hand-illustrated and hand-bound, price one cent (two copies, one remainder). The "K" circumflexed over the "night" was inserted by a brother ten years my senior. From the penny profit (from a sale within the family), I purchased a Mary Jane—taffy wrapped around a glob of peanut butter. Um.

Q. Then?

A. Shortly thereafter, I wrote, hand-printed, hand illustrated and hand-bound *Hawk Eye the Indian Boy* (two copies, price one cent, one remainder) which bought me another Mary Jane.

Q. And?

A. There followed a production entitled *The Sheriff of Red Roach Ranch*. ("Roach" was the spelling of my wicked older brother when I asked him if "Rock" was spelled with two "Ks." No matter.) I copied the spelling "Sheriff and "Ranch" from a book I was reading. Again, the one cent sale (leaving one remainder) paid for another Mary Jane.

Thus I conceived a notion.

Born was the idea that by writing I could eat.

That idea served as an apothegm for my subsequent career as a writer—a ruling not invariably a truism. As it eventuated there were times when I had Thanksgiving dinner at bottom of the totem pole at a hot dog stand.

However, I wrote many yarns for my high school magazine-an effort that caused an English teacher to suggest I submit a fiction effort to a magazine. Not overly optimistic, I knew I couldn't compete in a try for that day's top, the *Saturday Evening Post*. So I picked a pulp—*NorthWest Stories*. Luck! A check for $40.00! And a request for another story. This first story, "The Duel," would appear in the September 1926 issue.

That did it.

It was summertime, and I'd been a temporary P.O. employee peddling mail on a route on Long Island. With a high school buddy similarly employed, who shared room and board. And I had just carried a very heavy parcel-post package addressed to a "Tillie Tisswisser," 8,001 some local avenue at the end of the line. After lugging it an extra half mile, I discovered there was no such address. Belatedly suspicious, I pried open one corner of the package and exposed a cinder block. Which my pal had wrapped and mailed with a slew of cancelled stamps.

That would have done it if my check hadn't come that day with $40.00. "I quit! I just made a fortune!" I told them at the P.O. where I dumped the cinder block. (And I got even with my buddy by ducking out of our boarding house by letting my suitcase out of our bedroom window on a clothes line and leaving him stuck with the rent.)

Anyway, the $40.00 check started me on what eventuated as a career, writing for *Action Stories, Argosy, Short Stories* and *Adventure,* for such astute editors as Jack Byrne, Don Moore and, after the war (World War II), Burroughs Mitchell and Bud Hart. Of whom I still see Bud Hart—the others no longer among those present.

World War II pretty much killed most of the now extinct pulps. From paper shortage? I can't say. But many pulp writers faded away during the war. Among them, one of the best. Frederick Faust ("Max Brand"). I'm not certain, but I believe he may have been killed at Anzio.

If one finds some astonishing names among the early pulp editors some of the writers are equally surprising. In the early *Argosy-All Story.* Mary Roberts Rinehart, Octavus Roy Cohen, Zane Gray, E. Phillips Oppenheim, John Buchan. (Buchan, who wrote "The Thirty-Nine Steps," became Governor-General of Canada.)

Theodore Roscoe

ONE OF the questions often asked me is how did I happen to write about an old veteran yarn-spinner who spun yarns about his service in the French Foreign Legion. In North Africa back in the early '30s I encountered on a street in Casablanca this old-time Legionnaire with hashmarks up to his elbow. He agreed to talk over wine at a *brasserie.*

He didn't wear the classic old-time Legion uniform-the button-back blue overcoat, white trousers, blue cummerbund, heavy desert-boots called *brodequins.* He wore an old artillery-man's outfit. But the square-brim *kepi* with the gold torch insignia was Legion.

Questioning him in my limping French, and struggling to comprehend his metaphors, I got a *formidable* story. Aside from obvious hyperbole and manifest adjectives, some of it was perhaps true.

Here was my prototype for Thibaut Corday. Which, of course, wouldn't be his right name. You could enlist in the Legion under any name you chose, and since his right name was Hyacinth Rastagouch, he chose Corday for what is called a *nom de guerre.* Which became your official name as a "Stepson of France." Meaning you couldn't be extradited for a crime committed elsewhere—a fact, it was said contributed to the enlistment of numerous criminals using an alias. Who knows?

Because Frenchmen can't enlist in the French Legion, I had Corday say he was a Belgian. Or was it a Swiss? Anyway, the teller of my story attributed to Corday good English, partly translated.

Since his yarns were obviously mixtures of fact and fiction, I never presumed they would be taken seriously by the reader. And was surprised when several critics wrote to tell me the military tactics in this or that Corday tale were hokum. They were so intended to sound.

Incidentally, some Legion veterans in New York voted me an honorary member of the Veterans of the French Foreign Legion.

Actually, I never saw the Legion in combat. At a Legion H.Q. back in Sidi Bel Abbes, I was querying one of the officers. Apparently he thought I was planning to enlist. He shook his head at me with the comment: *"Discipline terrible!"* They followed the old rule, *"March qu creve."* "March or die." If a Legionnaire fell out, exhausted, in a Sahara march, they sent a sharpshooter back to kill him, and spare him from torture by desert tribesmen. But the Legionnaires I saw in action weren't risking their lives.

In Europe back then there was a saying. When the English conquer a country they build a custom house. The Germans build a fort. The French build a road. Back then (the '30s) the Legionnaires I saw in action were covered with not-very-glamorous dust, wielding picks and shovels building a road. Some of them in barracks slept in cots with the cot-legs in cans filled with water, to defeat scorpions. Their pay, if I recall correctly, afforded them a daily bottle of *pinard* (cheap red wine). Nothing so intriguing, colorful and lively as in such novels as *Beau Geste.*

So don't join the French Foreign Legion today. You'd get a plain khaki uniform, and risk only being bored to death.

Still, you'd learn one thing. Watch them, if chance occurs, on parade in France or on TV. There's no military outfit anywhere that can out-march their particular step.

ASIDE FROM the Foreign Legion, I most enjoyed writing for *Action Stories* a series about an adventurer named Peter Scarlet. There were at least 14 Peter Scarlet stories, beginning with "Jungle Joker" in the May 1927 issue of *Action Stories*. Other favorites were a tale entitled "On Account of a Woman" (*Adventure*, January 1936) and a tale for *Argosy*, "The Voodoo Express" (October 10,1931).

On another tack, I enjoyed writing a series for *Argosy* titled "Four Corners," which began with "He Took Richmond" in the June 5, 1937 issue of *Argosy*. These were adventures experienced by a youngster whose uncle was Sheriff in a small town about 100 miles from New York. One of the early Four Corners stories was "I Was the Kid With the Drum" (October 30, 1937)—a murder mystery. They used to have a kid aid the drummer by carrying in a parade the front end of a big base drum (guess where the body was concealed in a hurry by the murderer in this case). Of course, the drum seemed heavier than usual. And the drum-beat seemed more of a thump than the usual vibratory boom. The kid in the story didn't get it. But anyway the murderous drummer discovered he'd killed the wrong person.

In another "Four Corners" tale, I had a thief change his money into coins—loot he could bury in a well. Okay? But when he went back to safely get and spend this big bag of coins, he was trapped by the fact the silver dollars all bore the same date—the date of the robbery.

In one of my favorite Four Corners stories, "Frivolous Sal" (*Argosy*, July 17, 1937), the small town gentry were worried because it was rumored the young woman, so named (after a popular song), kept a diary. Fruitless efforts were made to get hold of it. In the end? Try to guess it.

I had a lot of fun writing "The Head," which appeared in *Short Stories*, December 10, 1932. As a stringer reporter, I had gone to Panama to investigate rumors of "White Indians" in the remote interior near the Colombian border. At a bar in Cristobal I asked the bar-keep if he'd heard of these Indians. Overhearing my query, a bar-fly character asked if I was interred in Jiboro Indians—the tribe that, through a mysterious process, boned, cured and somehow shrank human heads to the size of a base-ball. (Origin of the term "head-shrinker" for a psychologist.) The bar-fly said he had one to sell, and produced what appeared to be a much-shrunken human head. As the Jiboro Indians actu-ally beheaded their enemies and with incredible artsy-crafty skill created such curiosities, I was interested in the specimen handed me by the bar-fly. Ah! Only $300.00.

But the bartender, behind his hand, winked at me a negative signal. I didn't buy the head.

When the bar-fly indignantly took off with his allegedly shrunken head, the bartender advised me it was a fake, a monkey head fixed up to look human.

Later I saw an authentic shrunken head on display in another bar.

When World War II put an end to my pulp efforts, by good luck I sold *Only in New England*—a novel I'd intended for *Argosy*—to Scribner's. Surprisingly, it made the Literary Guild Book of the Month.

Thereafter, I wrote two Navy histories—*U.S. Submarine Oper-ations, World War II* (1949) and *U.S. Destroyer Operations, World War II* (1953) which were published by the Naval Institute at Annapolis (and are still on the market). I also wrote *This is Your Navy* (1950) for service reading. This was followed by *The Web of Conspiracy* (1959), about the Lincoln assassination, which became a *DuPont Show of the Month* on TV in 1961. Of which, with a great deal of help from my devoted wife, Rosamond, got me going again in fiction.

Today I can't recall what some of these tall tales written 50 years ago were about. Maybe I should have written some of them under an assumed name. But when I wrote them I felt I should take my lumps if, compared to many of early *Argosy's* great writers, my efforts proved mediocre. And on the other hand, if some drew plaudits, I'd like to take a bow in person.

Brave, no?